DANNY ORLIS
AND THE
ORDEAL AT CAMP

DANNY ORLIS
AND THE
ORDEAL AT CAMP

BERNARD PALMER

Aneko Press Youth

www.anekopress.com

Aneko Press, Life Sentence Publishing, and our logos are trademarks of Life Sentence Publishing, Inc.
203 E. Birch Street
P.O. Box 652
Abbotsford, WI 54405

JUVENILE FICTION / Religious / Christian / Action & Adventure
Paperback ISBN: 979-8-88936-012-4
eBook ISBN: 979-8-88936-013-1
10 9 8 7 6 5 4 3 2 1
Available where books are sold

CONTENTS

Ch. 1: Do I Have To?..1

Ch. 2: You're Mine! 11

Ch. 3: Look Who's Here! 19

Ch. 4: A Little Bird Told Me 27

Ch. 5: Putting Out the Bait 37

Ch. 6: That's Too Risky! 45

Ch. 7: We're Trapped! 55

Ch. 8: It's All Your Fault! 63

Ch. 9: Can't You Make Him Understand?............77

Ch. 10: Lost in the Middle of Nowhere.............89

Ch. 11: Clutching at a Straw 99

Ch. 12: Is This My Call for Life?.......................107

CHAPTER 1

DO I HAVE TO?

It was almost midnight, but Danny and Kay Orlis had not yet gone to bed. They sat quietly in the living room looking at one another.

"Linda Penner's a rebellious, headstrong girl, Kay," Danny began at last. "And I'm going to have to be gone a lot. Maybe we'd better tell Henry we can't keep her and Becky this summer."

"Oh, Danny," Kay's hand flew to her mouth, "we can't do that! We've got to help him and Linda. We can't turn our backs on them now. They need us all the more."

"I suppose you're right." Danny frowned thoughtfully.

"I almost wish she were a boy," Kay admitted after a time.

"That would just change the problem. It wouldn't make it any easier."

"If Linda were a boy, you could take her with you a lot of the time."

Danny picked up a picture that was sitting on an end table and held it in his hand. "You know, Kay, that just might be our answer."

She eyed him curiously.

"There's a Bible camp up in Canada where we could take Linda for the summer," he continued. "It's in a remote area, but it's a wonderful camp."

"Do you think it would be fair to unload our problem on the camp director?"

"I didn't tell you the whole story. The last time I flew in up there I met the camp director. He asked me to be on the lookout for someone who could help him with the counseling. I think he'd be very happy to have you and the kids come and stay for the summer. You could be chief counselor or take some other responsibility that would be a big help. Jim and Linda could probably help around the camp."

Kay thought for a moment. "Linda would be in a place where she couldn't be running with the wrong crowd," she admitted, "and the association with Christian kids would be a big help."

"I really think it would be best for all of us."

The following morning Danny sent a message to the camp director of the Northern Saskatchewan Bible Camp before going to work. A couple days later he had a reply. Only then did he tell the Penner girls and Jim Morgan about the plans for the summer.

"It looks as though I'm going to have to be away quite a lot this summer, so we thought it would be a good idea for Kay and you kids to go up to the Bible camp for the summer."

Jim could scarcely believe it. "You've been fishing up there, Danny. Is it as good as everyone says?"

"It's even better. You'd think I was making up something if I told you about the fish we caught the last time. And I understand that the lake beside the camp has as good fishing as practically any lake in the province."

The boy's eyes sparkled.

Linda, who had been listening to the conversation without comment, drew herself up. Her mouth was hard and twin flames of anger flickered in her dark eyes.

Danny Orlis didn't see the storm signals but, turning to her, remarked, "Well, Linda, it sounds as though Jim is sold on the plans for the summer. How about you? What do you think about going to Canada?"

Linda's face went ashen and her lips curled bitterly. "If you really want to know what I think, I think it's stupid."

The young missionary's expression did not change, and he did not raise his voice. "Those are harsh words, young lady. Just what have you got against camp?"

Tears trembled uncertainly beneath her eyelids. "I don't care! I meant every word I said!" Her voice rose. "I think it's a positively horrible idea. Who ever heard of spending all summer in a stupid Bible camp? I'd just as soon be in jail!"

Danny contradicted her with a smile. "Now wait a minute, Linda. I've been around this camp, and I happen to know that there's something going on every minute. You won't be bored; I'll guarantee you that."

She tossed her shoulders in defiance. "I know I won't be bored at that stupid Bible camp because I'm not going." With that she pushed back from the table, leaped to her feet, and went almost running to her room. For the space of a minute or two the others at the table looked at one another in silence.

Jim was the first to speak. "Wow, is she crazy! A chance to go to a great camp for all summer and she acts like that. What's wrong with her, anyway?"

Kay got to her feet. "I think I'll go and talk to Linda."

Linda was sitting by her bedroom window in the dark. "If you're going to try to talk me into going to camp with you, it won't do any good. I don't care what you say. I'm just not going."

Kay went over to the dresser and sat down on the bench near the angry girl. She did not speak for a minute or two, and Linda began to squirm.

"You and Danny always do everything just the way you want to around here," she pouted. "You never ask me if I happen to like your plans or not. You treat me like a baby."

Kay reached for the switch on the bed lamp, but changed her mind and left the room dark. When she spoke she chose her words carefully. "Now, Linda," she began, "you know that Danny and I always take you girls and Jim into consideration when we make plans. We want you to be happy. We want what is the very best for you."

The girl snickered. "You say that, and you try to make everybody believe it, but you can't fool me. I know better. You hate me. That's why you try to plan things that you know I don't like. You just hate me!"

"Now, Linda," Kay replied, "you know better. Danny and I love both you and Becky as much as if you were our own children. We want you to be happy, but we must also insist that you be obedient."

Linda began to sob uncontrollably. "You say you love me," she mumbled, "but if you really did you wouldn't want to make me go up to that stupid old Bible camp and stay all summer when you know that I'm going to hate it."

Kay spoke gently, but there was a firmness in her voice. "I don't see how you can be so sure you won't like it, Linda. You've never been there. You don't even know what it's like."

The crying became weaker. "Maybe I haven't been to that camp," she admitted, "but I've been to other camps lots of times. They're the most boring, most miserable places that I–I've ever known. I hated every minute I've ever been to a camp and this one won't be any different than the others." Tears trembled in her young voice.

"I don't know about the camps that you've been to, Linda," Kay told her, "but I do know that I had some wonderful times at camp when I was a girl. I still look forward to going to camp." She paused a moment. "If you go to this camp in Canada with the right attitude, it can be the most enjoyable time of your life."

By this time Kay's eyes had become used to the darkness until she was able to see the pout on Linda's lips.

"Camp may be the place where you'll see that your life lacks purpose and direction because you've never confessed your sins and put your trust in the Lord Jesus Christ." She leaned forward and her voice lowered earnestly. "This is the reason you're having all the trouble you've been having, Linda. Satan rules your life, and the Holy Spirit is convicting you of sin. You're upset and unhappy because God is dealing with you."

The girl straightened suddenly and her voice was harsh. "There you go preaching again!" she snapped hotly. "All you ever do is preach at me! Well, I can tell you this much: it's not going to do you any good. I don't care what you say to me, I'm not going to that stupid camp. I–I'd rather die first!" With that a wild sob escaped her lips and she began to cry uncontrollably.

Kay was not swayed by the sudden outburst. For a minute or two she sat quietly in the bedroom and allowed Linda to cry. When she spoke, it was with sympathy, but with a certain sternness that surprised the girl on the bed because Linda had always supposed that Kay could be "cried" into anything. "I'm sure that you'll feel differently about camp in the morning, Linda," Kay assured her evenly. "Good night."

As soon as the door closed behind Kay, Linda

stopped crying and sat up on the bed. "I'm not going to camp!" she exclaimed forcefully under her breath. "I don't care what they say! I'm not going to any dumb old camp where I can't have fun!"

The following morning Linda Penner said nothing at all about camp at the breakfast table, and no one else mentioned it. However, she had not forgotten about it. That afternoon, as soon as school was out, she called her dad's employer and found out that he would be coming back to Fairview that night. "This is Linda," she began. "Would you please tell Dad that I've got to see him right away? It's terribly important."

Her dad's boss was concerned. "You sound upset, Linda. Is there something wrong? Is there something I can do?" She hesitated. "I just want to talk to Dad," she answered. "Tell him that I've got to see him right away, but that I can't talk to him at the place where Becky and I are staying. I want to see him alone."

As soon as Henry Penner got the message that evening, he came over to the Orlis home and picked up Linda. Concern shone in his tired eyes. "Now, Linda," he commenced. "What's this all about?"

"I–I miss you so much, Daddy. I wish that we could be together again."

He was sorrowful and sympathetic. "I miss you and Becky, too. There's nothing that I'd like better than to be able to have you girls back with me again."

She eyed him carefully. "We can be together again, Daddy – just the three of us."

"You know that isn't possible," he told her. "You girls have to have someone to look after you while I'm gone. I'm just thankful that you have a good Christian home like Danny and Kay's to stay in."

She sniffled a little – quietly. "I know you think it's wonderful to have us over at Danny and Kay's," she murmured. "They're good friends of yours and everything. You–you probably wouldn't believe me if I told you what it's really like."

The corners of his mouth tightened. "What wouldn't I believe?"

"Danny and Kay make everyone believe that they're such good Christians, but you–you ought to see them when they're at home and think no one can hear them. You and M-m-mom never used to fight that way."

Her dad frowned. "Fighting doesn't sound like Danny and Kay. They seem to be too level-headed and to love each other too much for that."

Linda sat up straight. "That's only because you don't know them the way I do, Daddy," she protested. "When Danny gets mad you just ought to hear him!" She took a deep breath. "And as far as Danny goes, I think he just hates me."

"Now Linda, honey, I'm sure you must be mistaken." He clumsily put his arm about her shoulder. "It's just that you're lonesome for me and–and your mom. You don't really feel that way."

"Oh yes I do." Her voice broke. "I've tried to like to

stay with Danny and Kay. I've tried to do the things they want me to do, but it seems as though I can't do anything right." She started to cry again. "It doesn't make any difference what happens, I get blamed for it. Jim Morgan doesn't have to do a thing around the house, and I have to work all the time. . . ."

Her father's face darkened. "You're sure you're not making this up?"

Her gaze met his. "I–I didn't think you'd side with them against me, Daddy," she moaned.

"I'm not siding with anyone against you, honey," he answered, "but this puts me in a terrible spot. I can't leave you and Becky alone. I've got to have someone to look after you two while I'm out of town."

She dabbed at her eyes. "I'm almost fifteen and you know that I can cook and clean house. I'd take good care of Becky; honestly, I would. I'd do as well as Kay does. And I'd promise you that I wouldn't do a single thing you wouldn't want me to do."

But her dad was unmoved. "There's no use for you and me to be talking about this, Linda. I've got to have someone to look after the two of you. I'm away from home two or three nights a week. I'd have to quit my job if you were staying with me."

Linda's eyes blazed. "Do you know what Danny and Kay want me to do this summer? They say they're going to make us go up to Canada to some stupid old Bible camp with them. They're going to make me go along and work – all summer."

"Danny talked with me about that the other day before he wrote to the camp director," her dad replied. "It sounds like a great idea to me. You ought to have a wonderful time."

She looked at him appealingly. "I would have a wonderful time if you were going along, Daddy," she told him. "It would be wonderful then. But I'll be so lonesome for you that I won't be able to stand it."

"You won't be alone. You'll have Becky with you." Linda reached over and laid a hand on her father's arm. "Daddy, Danny and Kay both like Becky a lot. They let her do almost anything. And she–she likes to be with them. I'm the one they're mean to. Why don't you let me come home and live with you? Let me come back for the summer and take care of the house. We'll be together – just the two of us."

Henry Penner hesitated.

"Please?"

CHAPTER 2

YOU'RE MINE!

Henry Penner took a deep breath and expelled it slowly. For a moment or two he did not look at his daughter.

"Won't you please let me come home and keep house for you this summer, Daddy?" Linda continued pleadingly. "I won't cause you any trouble. Honestly, I won't. I'll go to church and Sunday school every Sunday and youth group and prayer meeting and–"

When her father spoke, his voice was harsh with anger. "I don't know why it takes me a long time to get angry, but it does. I think I'll go over and talk to Danny Orlis man to man. There's got to be something wrong or you wouldn't feel the way you do about staying with them. I'm going to find out what it is."

Fear flickered in her dark eyes and for a moment or two indecision and uncertainty reflected in her face. "W-w-what are you going to say to him, Daddy?"

"Plenty. I'm going to ask him what this is all about. I'm going to tell him how you came crying for me to take you home. I'm going to find out why he's been mistreating you."

"I–I wish you wouldn't," she stammered. "It–it'll make things so much worse for me if I do have to stay with them. He'll be real nice to you and then when you're gone he'll take it out on me. Both Danny and Kay will take it out on me." Her small fingers tightened on his arm. "Why don't you just let me move back home with you, Daddy? We could try it for this summer and if it doesn't work out, I'll go back to Danny and Kay's and not say a word. You'd soon find out that you can depend on me."

"I just might do that," he answered.

Linda brightened noticeably. "Then it's all settled?"

"I've got to talk to Danny and Kay first. I'm going to get to the bottom of this."

Linda Penner's face became pale. "It won't do any good to talk to them. Th-they'll just deny it."

Her dad did not answer her until they stopped in front of the Orlis home. "I'll get to the truth." He opened the car door, but she remained seated. "I–I think I'll just wait out here," she stammered.

"You'd better come inside with me."

Danny came to the door in response to the knock and held out his hand warmly. "Hello, Henry. How are you?" Mr. Penner did not take his hand. "Linda and I want to talk to you, Danny," he said icily.

"Sure thing. Won't you come in?"

"If it's all the same to you, we'd rather talk out here."

Danny came out on the porch and closed the door behind him. "You seem disturbed, Henry," he observed. "What's the trouble?"

"Linda tells me that you've been mean to her." His voice was half a question, half an accusation.

"Mean to her?" Danny echoed. "I don't believe I follow you, Henry. We've tried to treat her as we would treat our own daughter."

Linda shifted from one foot to the other uneasily.

"Linda says you let Jim Morgan get away with anything he wants to," Henry continued, "but if she even looks as though she's doing something wrong you pounce on her. She says you don't like her and pick on her all the time."

Danny turned to the ashen-faced girl. "Linda, suppose you tell your dad the truth." His voice was quiet and unruffled.

Henry Penner broke in quickly. "I didn't come over here to talk to Linda. I came to talk to you."

"I'd rather have her tell you just what the situation is. It's true that we've punished her, Henry. We've had to. She has continually told us things that weren't true and has deliberately disobeyed us. We have had to punish her."

Linda's gaze was fixed on the porch floor. "I–" she stammered.

Her dad looked down at her piercingly. "Is this true, Linda?" he demanded.

"I–I didn't exactly lie to Danny and Kay, and–and I didn't mean to disobey them, either. But Danny and Kay always think the worst of me. If Jim tells them something, or Becky, they believe them, but if I tell them something they always act as though I–I'm lying."

"I think you've said enough already." Mr. Penner turned to Danny Orlis. "I'm sorry for getting all upset like this. I should have known better."

"That's quite all right," Danny answered. "I really should have talked with you about this before."

Henry turned to his daughter. "Go to your room, Linda," he commanded firmly. "I want to talk to Danny."

For a brief instant hope gleamed in her eyes. "Are you going to talk about taking me back home to live with you this summer?" she asked.

He shook his head. "Decidedly not. You're going up to Canada with Danny and Kay. I wouldn't dare trust you at home without supervision."

Pouting, Linda Penner went into the house.

* * *

The next afternoon the phone rang at the Orlis home and Linda answered it.

"Is that you, Linda?" her friend Betty began. "There's someone here who wants to talk to you."

A moment later she heard a familiar voice. "Hi, Kitten."

Her young voice froze. "Jack Ross. What do you want?"

He laughed. "I want to talk to you, and I was afraid one of your jailors would answer the phone, so I had Betty do the calling."

"I don't know that I want to talk to you," she told him stiffly.

"Now what's the matter?"

"You know very well what is the matter, Jack."

"If you're talking about the other night," he snickered, "forget it. I was just trying to have a little fun."

The corners of Linda's mouth twitched, but she said nothing.

"Linda, are you still there?"

"What do you want?"

"I just want to talk to you," he repeated. "Is there any law against that?"

"If you're going to talk, you'd better hurry. Kay Orlis will be back in a couple of minutes."

"I hear by the grapevine that you're going away for the summer."

"Going away?" she exclaimed bitterly. "I'm going to be shipped to Siberia."

"That's too bad, Kitten. I had big things planned for you and me for this summer."

"Maybe you'd better find someone else."

Anger tinged Jack Ross's voice. "Listen," he snapped, "if I wanted to find someone else, that's just what I'd do; I don't need you to tell me. But I happen to want to be with you, Kitten. Understand?"

In spite of herself, a smile crept over her face. "It doesn't make much difference. We're going to be leaving the first thing in the morning."

"That's why I had Betty call you today. I've got to see you before you leave."

Linda looked about. "There's not a chance for that," she sighed. "Dad is coming over to say goodbye to us tonight. I wouldn't be able to get out of that."

"What are you doing right now?"

She hesitated. "N-n-nothing."

"Good. Come right down to the snack shop. I'll be waitin' for you."

For an instant or two after Linda Penner hung up, she stood there uneasily. She had promised herself that she would never go out with Jack Ross again – that she would never even speak to him. But he was sort of exciting, and he did like her. After all, not every freshman girl could go out with an upperclassman who had one of the coolest cars in school.

She hurriedly combed her hair and left the house and went down to the shop. Jack Ross was waiting.

"Hi, Kitten," he greeted her, grinning almost triumphantly. "Long time no see."

She glanced over her shoulder, fearful that someone would spot them together. "Let's go back to a booth, Jack," she began uncertainly. "I–I don't dare to stand out here and talk to you."

He laughed. "So you won't be seen with me? Is that it? That's a good one. Guess I'm getting quite a 'rep' since I was picked up by the cops on the way home from Forest City."

She did not answer.

He guided her back to a booth and sat down across from her.

"What did they do to you, Jack?" she asked. "At the trial, I mean."

He grinned. "Nothing. Why should they?"

"But I thought–"

"Oh, my old man had to go down to the judge and kick out a few hundred bucks to pay my fine, and the judge lectured me for about five minutes. But that was all there was to it. I didn't even lose my driver's license."

Linda Penner sighed deeply. "I was so worried."

"There wasn't anything to worry about. My old man was pretty mad for a little while, though. He said he was going to boil me in oil if I cost him another fine like that."

Linda spoke hesitantly. "It was a good warning not to drive so fast."

Jack snorted. "What do you mean, a warning not to drive so fast? That was just a warning not to get caught." Then he looked at her seriously. "You aren't going to have to be gone all summer, are you?" he asked.

"All summer," she told him, "and I hate every minute of it already."

"I don't blame you. That Danny and Kay Orlis really must be a couple of losers to expect you to spend all summer in church." He leaned forward and laid his hand on hers. "What's the matter with your old man? Why don't you talk to him about it? You don't have to take anything like that."

"You just don't know my dad." With a little sympathy she was beginning to feel sorry for herself again. "I tried to talk to him, but he believes everything Danny tells him."

"Well," Jack smirked, shrugging his shoulders, "it's going to be tough, but the summer won't last forever. And we'll make up for it when you get back in the fall. You're going to be my girl. Understand?"

She eyed him curiously. "What do you mean?"

"You and I are going to start dating, Linda," he told her confidently. "You're not going to go out with anyone else all year."

For an instant or two she could scarcely believe that he was even talking to her. "You–you mean you're asking me to date you?" she echoed.

He shook his head. "I'm not askin' you, Kitten. I'm tellin' you. From now on you're my girlfriend. You aren't goin' out with anyone else."

Linda walked home in the clouds. She was Jack Ross's girlfriend; he had said so himself. Forgotten was her anger over the way he had treated her on their last date. Forgotten was her resolve never to go out with him again.

If only she didn't have to go to that stupid Bible camp! Then everything would be perfect!

CHAPTER 3

LOOK WHO'S HERE!

That night Linda Penner found sleep long in coming. If only she could get out of going up to camp, everything would be wonderful. But there was no chance of that. And, as though it wasn't bad enough to make her go up there when she knew she was going to hate it, Danny Orlis wouldn't even let her wait until the second trip. He was taking Jim Morgan and Linda early the next morning while Kay and Becky got to wait at home for him to come back and get them. It was just because Danny hated her so much. He was just doing it for spite.

Linda's pretty young face clouded. She was mad enough to–to–to spit.

The flight to Northern Saskatchewan was both interesting and beautiful, but she had long since determined not to enjoy any of it. She sat in front with Danny and refused to look out, her gaze firmly fixed on the instrument panel.

Every now and then Danny glanced in her direction. She just hoped he saw how miserable he was making her.

After several attempts at talking to her, Danny lapsed into silence. It was not until they were nearing the camp that he spoke again.

"Well, Linda, we'll soon be there."

She snorted. "Big deal."

He circled the Bible camp on Lake Keewatin, settling down on the landing strip that served a nearby fishing resort. The light plane had scarcely stopped rolling before a tall, bronzed young man came hurtling up in a battered pickup. "Hi, Danny!" he sang out.

The young pilot climbed out of the plane and thrust out his hand. "Hi, Matt. It's good to see you. How're things going?"

"I think we're going to have a tremendous camp this year, Danny," the director told him. "Registrations are way up, and we've got a good, dedicated staff. We're looking forward to some wonderful times with the Lord."

Linda Penner sat in the front seat of the pickup with Danny and Matt Collins while Jim Morgan climbed into the pickup bed with the luggage.

The trail from the landing strip to the Bible camp crossed a small, sparkling-clear creek, skirted a corner of a small lake, and climbed over a series of hills to Lake Keewatin and the Bible camp. Danny was overwhelmed by the beauty all around them.

"I've lived in the north country almost all my life, Matt," he exclaimed, "but I think this is the most beautiful spot I've ever seen!" He looked Linda's way. "Isn't it beautiful?"

She acted as though she didn't know that he was talking to her until he spoke again and called her by name. Then she wrinkled her nose. "I wouldn't know."

Matt's and Danny's gazes met expressively.

Jim was as excited and happy as Linda was moody. At the camp he jumped out of the back of the truck and looked about, wide-eyed and smiling.

"Oh, wow!" he exclaimed. "Isn't this great, Danny?"

Matt came over to where he was standing. "Like it?" the camp director wanted to know.

"Like it?" he echoed. "I don't see how a person could help liking a place like this."

Linda had climbed out of the truck and remained motionless, a pout twisting her pretty young face. A moment later she turned to Jim. "Well," she asked, "are you going to get my suitcase for me, Jim, or do I have to climb up on that dirty old truck and get it myself?"

He laughed easily. "Keep calm. I'll get it for you."

The camp director turned to Linda. "If you'll wait here just a minute, Linda, I'll get your counselor. She'll show you to your cabin."

Danny and Matt Collins went off together and Jim began to take the suitcases out of the back of the pickup.

"Isn't it great that we got to come up here to stay all summer, Linda?" Jim asked. "This is going to be the best summer that we've ever had."

"Maybe it will be the best summer you've ever had, but I don't see anything so great about it." She took a long, deep breath. "As far as I'm concerned, it looks like a horrible place."

He stopped what he was doing and stared at her in amazement. "Now I've heard everything!" he exclaimed. "You'd probably complain if someone gave you a gold-plated convertible."

Before she could say more an attractive young woman in a heavy sweater came striding up to them. She was younger than Kay Orlis, but had that same gentle air and look of quiet assurance. Her smile was warm and inviting. "Hello, Linda," she greeted her. There was a trace of accent in her voice.

"Hello." Linda spoke grudgingly, as though she wouldn't have said anything at all had she had a choice.

"My name is Wilhelmina," the older girl told her, "but the girls all call me Wil."

Linda did not reply, but that did not seem to bother her counselor particularly.

"We're so happy to have you in our cabin."

"I'm not happy to be there," she grumbled under her breath.

Wil's smile broadened. "Wouldn't you like to see where you'll be staying?" she asked. "I may be prejudiced, but I think we have the best girls and the most beautiful location in all the camp."

She started to pick up Linda's suitcases, but Jim beat her to them.

"Here," he said. "Let me do that."

"Thank you."

They all started up the little hill toward the cabin together. It was a minute or two before Jim spoke again.

"You talk sort of different, Wil," he blurted. "Is your home in Canada?"

She shook her head. "My home is in Amsterdam, Holland. I'm here to go to Bible school."

Jim looked at her almost with wonder. "Wow, I've never met anyone from Holland before."

Forcefully Linda caused her frown to deepen. She didn't care if Wil was from Holland and seemed so kind and happy. She wasn't going to like her. She wasn't going to like anything at all about Bible camp. That was for sure.

At the cabin door Jim set the suitcases down. "I sure would like to talk to you some time when you're not busy," he requested. "I'd like to find out some things about Holland."

Wil's smile was genuine. "I'd like to talk to you, too."

When Jim was gone Wil turned to Linda. "It's swim time and the other girls are down at the lake. If you'd like to take a quick look at the cabin, I think you'd still have time to go swimming."

Linda wrinkled her nose. "No, thank you," she answered coolly.

"Well, come on in and I'll show you your cot."

Linda allowed herself to be led into the large cabin and taken to one of the narrow cots in the far corner of the room.

"This is yours, and this is your clothes closet." She giggled good-naturedly. "There's plenty of room to hang your things. We each have two hangers and two nails."

Disgust was written on Linda's face. Wil noticed it immediately.

"Your eyes are sad, Linda," she observed. "Is something wrong, no?"

"I thought at least I'd get a bed near a window. After all, I'm stuck in this dump all summer."

Wil's smile broadened. "So am I," she confessed, "and I love it."

The counselor sat down on the bed and motioned to Linda to sit down across from her. Slowly the American girl did as she was bidden.

"You are not happy to be here, are you, Linda?"

The corners of the girl's mouth tightened. "What makes you say that?"

"Lights don't shine in your eyes," Wil explained, "and your face is clouded. You can't be happy."

Linda bit her lower lip to keep from crying. "Who could be happy stuck in a crummy dump like this?" she demanded. The words exploded from the pain and anger in her young heart. "Bad enough to have to come here for a week, but I'm stuck for all summer!"

Wil spoke gently to her, keeping her voice down. "You know, Linda, there are times I have to go places I do not like to go, and have to do things I don't like to do. But I have learned that if I make up my mind to like it, I soon find out that I am having good times."

The younger girl's eyes flashed defiantly. "Don't you try to preach to me, too. Danny and Kay tried to sell me on all that stuff before we left home, but I'm not buying it. I might have to stay up here, but I don't have to like it! And I'm not going to do anything while I'm here. It won't do you, or anyone else, any good to try to make me!"

The counselor got to her feet. "I've got to go now, Linda," she said. "You will feel better tomorrow."

Linda Penner sat alone on her cot for several minutes. She never had any fun at camp, and this was worse than the others. She just knew it was going to be miserable.

That Wil didn't need to think she was going to soft- soap her into going out with the other kids and taking part in the camp activities. She probably hated her in the very same way that Kay and Danny did. She was just being nice because Matt Collins had told her.

Linda had made up her mind that she wasn't going to eat supper that night, but when the bell rang, she got her jacket and went with the other girls across the grounds to the dining hall. A vivacious red-haired girl about her own age came up beside her.

"Hi."

Linda glanced her way. "Hello." She spoke grudgingly.

"My name's Cherry Adams, and I live in Saskatoon."

Linda's face was expressionless. "What made you come up to a miserable place like this?" she asked.

Cherry eyed her curiously.

"This camp isn't miserable, it's wonderful." She paused. "I accepted Christ as my Savior last night."

A superior little smile twisted Linda's thin face. "So they hooked you," she mocked her. "That's nice. Now you can never have any fun."

The corners of the other girl's mouth tightened. "What do you mean?"

"Never mind."

Just then a gangling red-haired boy, a full head taller than Cherry, called out to her and waved carelessly. She waved back.

"Who's that?" Linda wanted to know.

"That's just Gregg. He's my brother."

"He's cute."

Cherry Adams' eyes widened. "Him?" Amazement crept into Cherry's voice. "You can't mean Gregg."

Linda smiled. "Maybe camp isn't going to be so bad after all," she told her.

CHAPTER 4

A LITTLE BIRD TOLD ME

Linda Penner stood beside her new friend thoughtfully, a faint smile momentarily chasing the pout from her lips. "It just could be that this might not turn out to be such a bad summer after all."

Cherry's eyes widened and her nose wrinkled. "You think my brother Gregg is cute? Are you sure you feel all right?"

"But he is cute," Linda protested. "He's got the prettiest red hair and adorable blue eyes and he–he looks so adult and so-so masculine. I think he's a doll."

Cherry snickered and Linda bristled slightly.

"Now, what's wrong with you?" she demanded.

"Nothing. I just got to wondering what he would say if he could hear you say that he's cute."

"You may find out." A dreamy look came to her dark eyes. "He must be absolutely stunning in a football uniform."

Cherry Adams shrugged her shoulders indifferently. "I wouldn't know. I don't think he ever played football in his whole life. Hockey's his sport."

Linda's smile broadened. "Now that is a coincidence," she cried. "I like football all right, but hockey's really the sport that I like the best."

Cherry grew serious. "Before you do a flip over Gregg I ought to warn you about him. He doesn't even know that girls exist."

Linda took half a step forward and her new friend touched her on the arm.

"Where are you going?" she asked.

"I just thought I'd sort of circulate around and see if I can get acquainted with some of the other kids."

She walked off, leaving Cherry Adams alone. The young Canadian girl's head was full of questions about this strange new friend whose name she didn't know.

The Bible camp kids were just lining up for dinner when Linda slipped into the line directly behind Gregg Adams. As she did so, she bumped his arm.

"Oh, pardon me," she said.

Startled, he turned, but before he could speak, she dimpled up at him.

"Hello." He was all she had thought he was and more. Much more. His shoulders were broader and there was a handsome cut to his bronzed square-chiseled features. The girls back home would swoon when they heard about him.

She spoke again. "My name's Linda Penner."

He eyed her indifferently. "Oh."

"And you're Gregg Adams."

His perplexity grew. "Am I supposed to know you or something?" he asked, pausing uneasily.

"You know me now." She laughed. "I was talking to your sister a little while ago. She told me all about you."

"Oh, you know the brat? Don't believe everything she tells you about me. She really gets in my hair."

By this time they had reached the stack of trays and plates that signified the beginning of the dinner line. "I didn't think I was going to like anything about this stupid old camp," Linda went on. "But it's like I was telling Cherry. I don't think it's going to be so bad – now."

"Yeh–" He could not have been more indifferent. He held his tray out to the girl behind the counter. "Have a heart, won't you? Give me another scoop of potatoes."

"You're always begging," she countered. "Last night you tried to talk me out of more beans."

"You wouldn't hold that against me, would you? I'm a growing boy. I've got to keep up my strength. Come on. You wouldn't want to starve me to death, would you?"

The girl laughed as she took his plate and put more potatoes on it. "I don't know why I let you talk me into giving you extra portions every night. It must be that I'm getting soft and easy to get around."

"Thanks." He grinned at her. "Thanks a lot. Know something? When I get me a girl, she's going to have to be just like you – with lots of potatoes and a big heart."

Linda followed Gregg toward the empty tables across the dining hall. "There's room for us to sit here, Gregg," she told him.

He frowned. "Yeh, there is. There is at that." He was looking around. After a moment his eyes brightened. "There are a couple of guys I want to see over there." He started away. "So long, *Martha.* I'll see you around." With that he crossed to the table where Jim Morgan and a number of guys were sitting.

Linda stared after him, flushing slowly. He hadn't even remembered her name! What was the matter with her, anyway? Why had she made such a fool of herself? She sat down alone and, in a minute or two, began to eat.

Gregg Adams was cute in spite of what Cherry said. He was almost as cute as Jack Ross. Probably every girl in camp, except his sister, would give a year's allowance to have a date with him. Gradually her color came back to normal, and her smile returned. Gregg Adams might not look at her now, but just wait. Just you wait!

* * *

The speaker at the campfire service that evening stirred Linda Penner in a way that she had never been stirred before. He was not polished or particularly gifted, but his message was simple and direct and filled with the Word of God.

"Jesus said, *You must be born again,*" the speaker quoted.

He turned and seemed to stare directly into Linda's heart. "Being born in a chicken coop won't make you a chicken," he continued. "Being born in a garage doesn't make you a car. Just so, being born into a Christian family won't make you a Christian.

"You can't get to heaven on the salvation of your father or your mother. You have to face up to the sin question personally. You must recognize that you are a sinner, confess your sin, and put your whole trust in the Lord Jesus Christ for salvation. Then, and then only, will you be a child of God. . . ."

Linda Penner squirmed uncomfortably. She was all right. There was nothing wrong with her. She was a Christian, even though she did like to have a little fun once in a while. Why, she had been going to church ever since she could remember, and she had gone through the Bible instruction class and everything. What more could they expect of her?

Still–still–

That night when the service was over Linda got slowly to her feet and looked about for some sign of Gregg Adams. She did not see her counselor until Wil put an arm affectionately about her shoulder.

"It was a nice service, wasn't it, Linda?" she asked.

The girl shrugged her shoulders. "When you've been to one, you've been to them all," she countered. "They're all alike. The speaker talks for thirty minutes and then spends another thirty minutes pleading with the kids to come forward."

If Wil was shocked, she gave no indication of it. "I've got to go over to Mr. Collins' cabin to get some material, Linda," she went on, "and it's such a beautiful night. I don't like to walk alone. You will go with me?"

The girl's lips parted as though to refuse, but the counselor smiled her protest away and took her by the arm.

"It is so wonderful to be here in a place like this – apart with God," Wil observed quietly as they walked slowly up the path.

Linda stiffened. "Now I suppose she's going to start in on me," she told herself defensively. "Well, it's not going to do her any good, I can tell you that much. Nobody's going to make a fool out of me over religion and ruin all my fun."

Surprisingly, however, the counselor said no more.

Linda saw Gregg Adams now and again during the next two or three days, but it was toward the end of the week before she got a chance to talk to him. She had just finished with one of the handcraft lessons and was heading back to the cabin to get her Bible when she saw him crouched tensely near a little clump of trees, staring at something intently.

A smile glinted in her eyes, and she took a few steps toward him. "Hello there."

"S-s-sh!" He put up a hand in warning.

"What are you doing?" she asked playfully, "playing hide-and-go-seek?"

A bird in a nearby tree flew away.

Gregg straightened and turned to face her, disgust

glinting in his eyes. "For cryin' out loud!" he exclaimed. "Do you have to keep blabbin' all the time?"

Anger whitened little circles in her cheeks. "All I did was speak to you," she told him. "What's so terrible about that?"

"All you did was speak to me," he repeated, "and chase away the only western wood peewee I've seen since we've been up here."

"What's a western wood peewee or whatever?" she asked him.

Gregg Adams' voice grew more animated. "A western wood peewee is a bird about six inches high. He's a little more gray than the eastern wood peewee and–" He broke off suddenly. "What's the matter with me? You aren't interested in birds."

"Oh, but I am," she assured him. "I just *love* birds. All kinds of birds."

He eyed her skeptically. "The only girl I ever saw around here who's interested in birds is Wil," he replied, " and she's not a girl. She's a counselor."

Linda left him soon and went up to her cabin. She had to see Wil right away. She had to find out something about birds. A smile broke across her face. It could be that this was just the break she needed.

Although she looked for the counselor for half an hour or so it was not until after dinner that evening that she got a chance to talk to her alone. "I was talking to someone this afternoon who said that you're interested in birds, Wil."

The counselor smiled knowingly. "You must have been talking to Gregg Adams," she answered, "the red-haired boy with the lights in his eyes."

Linda colored. "How did you know?"

"He's the only other person here at camp who has asked me about birds."

"I was talking to him," Linda admitted, "and he got me interested in birds. It sounds as though it would be a lot of fun learning about them."

"It is." Wil's smile was genuine. "And it is something anyone can do. All you have to do is get yourself a guidebook and go out in the woods and start looking around. You'll start seeing more different kinds of birds than you thought there were in the world."

Linda's eyes sparkled. "It sounds like a lot of fun. Would you help me get started?"

"Of course I will. Do you have a guidebook?"

"No, but I'll get one right away."

Linda went to talk to Kay that very evening about getting a guidebook on birds.

"That sounds like it would be interesting." Kay reached for her purse. "You know, it makes me want to do some bird watching again." She handed Linda some money.

Linda went to the snack shop, bought her guidebook, and sought out Wil. "I got my guidebook," she told her. "Can we get started?"

Wil took the book and opened it with interest. The smile softened her words. "What is the hurry, Linda?" she asked. "The birds will be here tomorrow."

"I know." Her cheeks colored delicately. "But you have me so interested I can hardly think of anything else."

"I have seen those lights in a girl's eyes before, but they were put there by a boy, not birds."

Linda wrinkled her nose. "The lights in my eyes weren't put there by a boy," she countered defensively. "I can tell you that much."

Wil scanned the last remaining pages and closed the book with finality. " I am afraid you bought the wrong book, Linda," she told her. "This is only about watching birds. It doesn't say anything at all about watching bird watchers."

Linda Penner frowned. "I don't know what you're talking about."

"It seems I see a red-haired bird watcher around here who has you watching him." She shook her finger jokingly. "You think Wil hasn't got eyes, but she has. She knows what's going on."

Linda flushed scarlet. "Just because I happened to stand in line and talk to Gregg Adams for a couple of minutes is no sign that I've fallen for him," she exclaimed.

"That's true, Linda. Yes, it is very interesting to study birds. It's more interesting to study the bird watchers."

A pout drooped Linda's lips. "I thought you were my friend. But you're just like all the rest."

Wil got up and went over to her. "That is all right, Linda, but if you want to learn about birds, we will learn about birds."

CHAPTER 5

PUTTING OUT THE BAIT

The next several days Linda Penner learned a great deal about birds from her counselor. She learned the names of the more common varieties in the area and how to identify them. And she learned the names and characteristics of a few less familiar. In the dining hall a few nights later she sought out Gregg Adams once more.

"Hello there." Her voice was as sprightly as her smile.

"Hello," he answered, looking about uneasily as though he was trying to find a way of escape.

"I saw a tanager this afternoon," she informed him.

"There are a lot of tanagers around here." His expression did not change. "You see them every once in a while."

"This one had red wings."

Gregg's interest was electric. "What did it look like?"

"It was all red like a cardinal – even its wings – only it didn't have a crest."

"A scarlet tanager way up here," he exclaimed interestedly. "What do you know! There aren't even supposed to be any this far north. The closest to us you're supposed to find them is southeastern Manitoba."

"Oh." Her voice was thin. That was one thing she hadn't noticed in the guidebook.

"But birds often go places where they don't normally live. Where did you see this scarlet tanager, Linda? And how long ago?"

She answered vaguely. "I–I don't remember just where I saw him, but it was on the campgrounds. I was in a hurry to go to class, and I don't remember for sure where I saw him."

"How long ago was it?"

She frowned as though trying to remember. "It was quite a while ago, Gregg. About the middle of the afternoon, I think. Or was it earlier? He–he wouldn't be there now."

"Oh, I know that," the red-haired bird watcher retorted. "But I sure wish you remembered where you last saw him. There may be a nest nearby."

"You–you might see him somewhere around the grounds," Linda continued, "if–if you keep looking for him."

"You be sure and keep looking for him, too," Gregg went on. "And if you see that scarlet tanager again or any other bird you're not too familiar with, remember where you saw him and when. I'd give a lot to get a picture of a scarlet tanager."

"Do–do you take many pictures?"

"Just some bird pictures. I've got a camera my uncle used to have and a telephoto lens. I make that sort of a hobby."

Linda sighed admiringly. "You've got so many hobbies, Gregg. You must lead an awfully interesting life."

His ears turned pink, and he started to shift from one foot to the other, nervously. "I–I've got to be going, Linda," he told her lamely. "If you see that scarlet tanager, be sure and let me know right away."

She went over to the place where Cherry Adams was sitting and pulled out a chair. That Gregg! All he could think about was watching birds. Why, he didn't even know that she was alive.

The messages at camp the next day or two were more challenging than they had ever been, and Linda squirmed with conviction. Every now and then it seemed as though the speaker was talking directly to her.

On one such occasion her counselor moved quietly over to her. "Linda," Wil whispered, "Linda, I believe the Lord is talking to you."

Head down, the girl gave no sign that she had even heard.

"His Spirit is talking to your heart," the counselor continued. "He is telling you that now is the time to confess your sin and trust Christ as your own personal Savior. Now is the time for you to get right with God."

Linda's head came up in defiance. "You don't have to worry about me. I'm all right."

"Before I confessed my sin and trusted Christ as my Savior, I used to try to tell people that I was all right, too. But down in my heart I knew that I wasn't. I knew that I was a wicked girl. I knew that I would go to hell if I died without trusting Christ as my Savior."

Linda's mouth was straight and as hard as iron. "Ever since I was as old as Becky, people have tried to scare me with talk like that," she retorted, "but I'd just as well tell you right now. It's not going to work. I'm a Christian, and I'm not going to be scared into making a fool of myself."

That night, however, Linda Penner tossed on her bed without going to sleep until the first faint gray streaks of dawn began to light the forest. She had told Wil she was a Christian, but was she? Had she really confessed her sin and put her trust in the Lord Jesus Christ?

She tried to talk to Gregg on several occasions during the next day or so, but he always seemed to be staring off into space or was in a hurry or something. He almost acted as though he was trying to keep out of her way.

"Sorry, Linda," he told her the following evening in the dinner line, "but I promised a couple of the guys that I'd eat with them. I'll be seeing you."

She tried, imperfectly, to mask her intense disappointment.

Then she and Wil heard about the eagle that was nesting in the area. They had gone out on the lake for a canoe lesson and had met an Indian who was going to the Hudson Bay store across the lake for supplies. An eagle flew overhead, a fish in its talons, while they were talking to the Indian.

He spoke slowly, "Eagle have nest. Feed young."

Instantly Wil was interested. "Do you know where the nest is?" she asked him.

"Over there." He pointed with a wide sweep of his arm. "On the island."

The counselor turned to Linda. "Now there is something that would be very interesting. We'll have to try to find time to go over and see it. They say that an eagle's nest is one of the most fascinating nests you'll find anywhere in North America."

Linda did not answer her. Already she was thinking of Gregg. This was luck! Wait until she told Gregg about this.

That night in the dining hall she looked for him. He was standing not far from Cherry. What a break that was, she told herself triumphantly, as she headed for her friend.

"Hi, Linda."

"Hello, Cherry." She smiled her sweetest.

"What are you so excited about?" Cherry wanted to know.

"You'd be excited, too, if you had been with me this afternoon."

The other girl eyed her curiously. "We missed you this afternoon. Where did you go?"

Linda lowered her voice, but took care to speak loudly enough so that Gregg would be sure to hear her. "An Indian showed us the location of an eagle's nest," she declared.

Cherry eyed her blankly. "An eagle's nest? Are you crazy or something? What's so wonderful about that?"

"An eagle's nest is just about the most interesting nest there is on the whole North American continent," she explained, parroting Wil's remark of a few hours earlier.

By this time Gregg had turned around and was facing Linda. "Did you really see an eagle's nest?" he demanded.

She smiled. "What's the matter, don't you believe me?"

"Sure I believe you," he answered, "but, I've been trying to find an eagle's nest ever since we came up here, but I haven't been able to. I've been wanting to get a picture of one."

She carefully widened her smile. "It's too bad you weren't with us this afternoon. You'd have had your chance."

Gregg's eyes gleamed. "How close did you get to it?"

"As close as you would want to. We had to keep a close eye out for the old eagle. They say they're awfully dangerous."

Gregg's excitement continued to grow. "Did the nest have eaglets in it?" he persisted.

At that moment she spied a friend standing half across the dining hall. "I'm sorry, Gregg, but I've got to go over and talk to Mary Jane."

"Just a minute, Linda," he protested almost frantically. "You haven't told me where the eagle's nest is or how to get there."

"The Indian said the old eagle got awfully nervous if anyone came around where the nest is," she told him. "He said he was afraid she might attack or something."

"You don't have to worry about me," he boasted. "I've done a lot of bird watching. I know enough to be careful."

She hesitated. "I–I'll have to think about it, Gregg. I practically promised that I wouldn't tell anybody about it." She had lied so often that apparently it didn't bother her at all. With that she left Gregg Adams standing there and walked, with exaggerated carelessness, across the dining hall to the place where a little knot of girls were visiting. Gregg eyed her wistfully, a fact that she was very pleasantly aware of.

That evening after the service Gregg started in her direction. She saw him coming and impulsively took hold of her counselor's arm.

"Isn't this a beautiful night, Wil?" she asked.

Together they walked up the path toward their cabin.

"You seem happy tonight, Linda," her counselor remarked. "The lights are in your eyes."

Linda shrugged her shoulders. "I wouldn't go so far as to say I was actually happy."

"You act as though you like camp better." Wil was studying her.

"I'm stuck here," she replied. "I figure that I'd just as well get a little enjoyment."

They walked a few yards in silence before Wil spoke again. "The red-haired bird watcher is watching you now, Linda," she reminded her slyly. "Has he given up on birds?"

The Penner girl bristled. "I don't have the slightest idea of what you are talking about."

"You can't fool me, young lady," Wil laughed. "Girls are girls in Holland, too. We have a few tricks, I tell you."

Linda only smiled.

"Only be sure you conduct yourself as a lady, Linda," her counselor warned. "And always be truthful with your boyfriends as well as other people."

Linda stopped short. "Just what kind of girl do you think I am, anyway?" she demanded.

CHAPTER 6

THAT'S TOO RISKY!

The following day Gregg Adams sought Linda Penner out on two or three occasions and begged her to tell him where to find the eagle's nest. "Come on, Linda, have a heart," he pleaded. "Just tell me where it is."

"I can't, Gregg," she protested. "I promised."

His eyes clouded. "Why did you have to promise a stupid thing like that?" he demanded.

"It doesn't seem like a stupid promise to me, Gregg. It seems very sensible."

"Well, it doesn't seem sensible to me," he retorted. "At least you could tell me where to find the Indian so I could go and talk with him about the eagle's nest myself."

"I don't know where the Indian is," she answered, irritably. "I don't know his name or anything about him."

Suspicion kindled in Gregg's eyes. "I don't think you even saw any Indian, and I don't think you saw an eagle's nest. You're stringing me along."

"Well!" Indignation tinged her voice. "If that's what you think, all right. Let's just forget that I said anything to you about it."

Before he could reply she stalked away.

Late that afternoon Danny Orlis flew in to spend the weekend at camp. Kay saw the plane first and ran down to the dock to meet him. He had only been in a couple of minutes when Jim Morgan came hurrying up to the plane.

"Hi, Jim," Danny called out. "How's it going?"

"Just great. This is some camp. I've never had so much fun in all my life."

Kay looked at her watch. "I'm sorry that I've got to run, Danny, but I've got a class in about five minutes," she mentioned.

"You go ahead. Jim'll help me tie down the plane and get my things up to our cabin."

When she was gone, Jim turned to Danny. "I'm sure glad we're alone, Danny," he told his guardian. "There's something I've got to talk to you about."

"What's the matter?" the youthful pilot asked him. "Some girl trouble?"

"I'll say that I have. Plenty of it." He leaned against the plane. "It's that Linda," he explained. "You've just got to do something about her."

"What's she doing now?"

"She's making a fool of herself and Kay and me," Jim said forcefully. "That's what she's doing." He straightened, his eyes flashing. "You just ought to see the way she's throwing herself at Gregg Adams.

Every time he turns around, there she is. He has to watch out to keep from knocking her down."

"Now, Jim, are you sure it's as bad as all that?"

"As bad as that?" His young voice grew louder. "It's worse, Danny. You ought to see her and the way she's been acting. The whole camp's talking about it. . . . Somebody's got to do something."

Danny said little to Jim, but at the first opportunity he talked with Kay about her.

"I'm afraid Jim's right, Danny," Kay Orlis agreed. "I've tried to talk to her, but it hasn't done a bit of good. She seems to spend most of her free time following that Adams boy around."

Danny was silent a moment. "I suppose I could talk to her, but I'm afraid she would just resent anything I said." His frown deepened. "Has she responded to any of the messages?"

Kay shook her head. "I'm afraid not. Sometimes I think a message is getting through to her, and the next time it just seems to be hardening her heart."

"We'll have to keep praying."

The day after Danny left to fly a missionary home on emergency furlough, Gregg sought out Linda again and talked with her about the eagle's nest.

"You've just got to tell me where it is."

She bristled. "I don't have to do anything," she countered defiantly.

"Come on, Linda." He took her by the arm. "You don't have to be so stubborn."

She moved away from him as if she had been injured. "I don't know how you can expect me to act any differently than I have been acting. First, you accuse me of lying to you. Then you tell me what I have to do. I'm not used to being treated that way."

He breathed deeply. "You know I didn't mean it that way."

She had trouble hiding a smile. "I haven't heard you apologize," she went on coldly.

"All right," he answered. "I apologize. I'm sorry I doubted you and I'm sorry I tried to tell you what to do. Now, will you tell me where that eagle's nest is?"

She wrinkled her nose at him.

"No."

"For cryin' out loud!" he exploded. "What do I have to do to get you to tell me where it is?"

"I can't tell you where it is," she said at last, "but I didn't promise not to show anyone where it is." She lowered her voice to a whisper. "I suppose I could take you there."

His eyes gleamed. "Would you?"

She nodded. "Tomorrow, maybe," she informed him coyly. "That is, if you're nice to me."

Gregg only heard the first of what she had said. "That'll be great! Wait 'til I tell Jim Morgan about that. He's going to be as excited as I am."

Linda frowned. "Jim Morgan?" she echoed. "What's he got to do with it?"

"Oh, I was telling him about the eagle's nest, and he decided that he wants to go along."

"He would." Linda's disappointment was apparent. "Do you have to take him?"

"Sure I've got to take him," Gregg countered. "Why wouldn't I? He's my best friend." He paused. "Besides, Jim's going to help me with the pictures."

"Well, if you say he has to go along I suppose it'll be all right," she finally agreed reluctantly. "But Jim Morgan's a pain in the neck as far as I'm concerned."

"How long is it going to take us to get over there?"

She rubbed her nose with her forefinger. "Not too long," she answered. "We ought to be able to make it during free time, easily."

"Good. I'll borrow a canoe from a friend of mine who's got a little place up the lake."

The next day Linda got Cherry Adams off to one side and asked her to go along.

"Why should I go along?" Cherry wanted to know. "I don't care about seeing an old eagle's nest."

"I know," Linda agreed, "but I don't want to go alone with two boys. It wouldn't look right." She lowered her voice. "Besides, we won't be gone very long. Not over an hour or two."

"Well–"

"Good!" the Penner girl exclaimed. "I knew you'd go with us."

The sun went under a heavy cloud cover just before noon. Jim didn't like the thought of taking pictures without the sun and wanted to wait, but Gregg would not hear of it.

"Nothing doing. We've got everything set now to go over there. I think that's what we'd better do."

"But you wanted pictures," Jim protested.

"After we find out where it is we can go back whenever we want to and get pictures and everything."

"That stupid Linda Penner," Jim said, disgust edging his voice. "She could just as well tell us where it is so you and I could go over there without her tagging along. But no, she couldn't do that, so we've got to drag her with us."

Instead of going out to their cabins to read or fool around the way most of the kids did during their free time, Linda and Cherry and Gregg and Jim slipped down to the beach and paddled away in the canoe Gregg had borrowed.

He frowned at his sister. "Who invited you to go along?" he demanded.

She wrinkled her nose at him.

"You're just going to weigh the canoe down," he told her. "I suppose you know that. It'll be just that much harder to paddle."

She looked at Jim. "You don't think I'm that heavy, do you?" she asked seriously.

His cheeks colored beneath the deep tan. Funny that he had never noticed Cherry Adams before. But she was cute. And she liked him – at least a little bit. If she didn't, that smile was sure deceiving.

"I'll paddle hard enough for you and me both."

"See." She turned to Gregg triumphantly. "I don't want to hear any more from you."

Gregg shook his head. "You'll be sorry, Jim. You don't know what you're letting yourself in for."

Linda eyed him impishly. "You know what that means, don't you, Gregg? It means you're going to have to paddle hard enough for you and me both."

"That's where you're wrong," he told her. "After we see the eagle's nest, I'm going to hand you the paddle and make you bring us back."

She made a face. This was going better than planned – much better.

She thought she knew exactly where the eagle's nest was after she and Wil had received the directions from the Indian. But the islands all looked so much alike. They went past one long narrow stretch of land, crossed the open water to another, and headed behind it. The wind was whipping the lake into choppy whitecaps and, every now and then, it looked as though it was going to rain.

Jim Morgan eyed the clouds uneasily. "We've been gone almost an hour, Linda," he reminded her at last. "Are you sure you know where that eagle's nest is?"

She looked about.

"I'm sure it–it–it–" She pointed suddenly. "Isn't that it over there?"

Jim turned to stare at her. "Linda Penner," he exclaimed hotly, "how stupid can you get! Eagles don't build nests in trees. They pick cliffs."

Gregg contradicted him, "Oh, no, Jim, that's where you're wrong. The golden eagle builds her nest on a cliff, but the bald eagle uses a real high tree."

Linda made a face at Jim. "See, I'm not as stupid as you think I am."

There, in the top of the tallest tree on the island, was the eagle's nest. Gregg thrust his paddle deep into the water and laid his weight to it. "That's it, all right," he said excitedly.

In a few minutes they had reached the island and were standing at the base of the towering pine tree.

Gregg turned to Jim. "Did you ever see a bird's nest like that?"

Jim shook his head. "I've always wanted to see an eagle's nest, but this is the first time I've had the chance."

"Do you think you can get the pictures we want?"

Jim surveyed the situation critically. "I don't see how we can get much of a picture from here," he answered, "unless we climb up there."

Cherry Adams' eyes widened fearfully. "You wouldn't dare."

Jim hid his pleasure at her concern. "I don't know," he continued. "It shouldn't be such a hard tree to climb."

He hadn't really planned on climbing, but with Cherry standing there. . . . He swallowed his fear.

"Give me your camera, Gregg. We can't get the picture we want from here."

Gregg handed him the camera and Jim started up the tree. Higher and higher he climbed while his companions watched breathlessly.

If only that big old eagle didn't come sailing in

about now! Jim Morgan caught his breath sharply while the strength drained from his body. A dark, fearsome shape was plummeting down at him from above, razor-like talons poised for the kill!

53

CHAPTER 7

WE'RE TRAPPED!

Cherry Adams screamed, "Jim! Look out!"

He scrambled half around the tree. And just in time! The eagle's wild dive missed him by inches. The big bird braked with her wings and banked to come about and renew the attack.

"Get down, Jim!" Gregg Adams shouted. "Hurry!"

Jim Morgan didn't need to be told. He slid from one branch to another, frantically.

The eagle slammed in at him, catching his shirt in her talons and ripping it to shreds. For a brief instant she hovered some ten or fifteen feet above him. Then, before he could move, she pounced again. This time she drove her talons deep into his shoulder.

Jim cried out in pain! For one terrifying moment he clawed for the tree. But the jerk of the great bird was too much for him. His hold on the branches gave way and he toppled backward, falling to the ground!

The eagle dove low over him before deciding that the threat to her nest and eaglets was over. Then, frantically, Gregg Adams and the girls ran to the place where he was lying.

"Jim!" Gregg cried. "Jim! Are you hurt?"

He groaned and moved, but painfully.

By this time Cherry and Linda were kneeling beside Gregg and were staring down at the prostrate boy.

Cherry was near tears.

"Jim!" she cried. "Are you hurt?"

Weakly he opened his eyes. "I–I didn't think she'd do that. I wasn't going to harm her nest."

"I shouldn't have let you climb up there," Gregg blurted. "I knew better. But I wanted those stupid pictures so bad." Gregg reached over and touched Jim's arm as though to help him sit up. The boy cried out in pain. "What's the matter?"

"I don't know." He spoke between clenched teeth. "I–I can't move my arm."

Linda Penner stood by helplessly. Cherry and Gregg cut Jim's torn shirt away to expose the bleeding gouges of the eagle's talons and his swollen, darkening forearm.

"I don't know much about first aid," Gregg admitted at last, "but I'm almost positive that your arm is broken, Jim."

The Morgan boy nodded grimly. Sweat stood out on his face and forehead and his entire body began to tremble.

Cherry Adams took over quickly. "We studied first aid in girls' club. I think Jim's going into shock."

Linda's breath was thin and shallow, and she was trembling almost as much as Jim was. "What does that mean?" she asked fearfully.

"It means that we've got to keep him warm," Cherry replied crisply. "We must get him back to camp quickly."

Jim opened his eyes and managed a weak little grin. "That was the most stupid thing I ever did," he grumbled. "Believe me, I now know better than to tangle with an eagle." A few drops of rain wet his face and the wind was freshening.

Gregg Adams peeled out of his sweatshirt. "We'll put this over Jim," he said. "We've got to get a move on. That storm's going to break any minute."

As though in answer to his words there was a sudden rush of wind and the heavens opened. Rain slanted down in great, driving sheets. The treetops groaned under the onslaught.

For a moment or two the young people huddled there, miserably, soaked to the skin.

* * *

Back at Bible camp Kay Orlis was also watching the storm. She glanced at the wind and rain and then turned to Matt Collins, the camp director.

"Matt," she inquired, "have you seen Jim and Linda?"

He shook his head. "They must be around here somewhere, though," he answered. "There's no place to go around here."

"Jim was supposed to have been in my last Bible class," Kay replied, "but he didn't show up. And that's not like him. He's always been as dependable as a good watch."

"Maybe he got caught in the storm somewhere and couldn't get back."

"That's not like him, either. As for Linda Penner, a person can never tell what she's going to do." Kay breathed deeply. "I can't help being a little concerned about them."

"I'm sure they're around the grounds somewhere," he attempted to assure her, "but as soon as the rain lets up a bit, I'll have a look."

Kay noted the time. "It won't be long until dark," she sighed.

* * *

On the other side of the lake Linda Penner started to whimper. "What are we going to do?" she asked. "We can't stay here."

Gregg Adams struggled to his feet against the force of the storm.

"Gregg!" Her voice was near hysteria. "You're not going to leave us!"

"I'll be back," he shouted. "I've got to go and see if I can find some shelter."

He was gone for only a few minutes, but it seemed like an hour or two. The girls huddled together near Jim Morgan.

At last Gregg came stumbling back to them.

"I didn't find much," he panted, "but I think we can get out of the wind."

Taking care to avoid bumping Jim's arm, Gregg helped the injured boy to his feet and over to a clump of brush behind a big rock. The girls plodded along behind.

Gregg spoke softly to Jim. "Feel all right?" he asked.

Jim shook his head. "I've never had anything hurt this bad," he whispered between clenched teeth.

"Don't worry. As soon as this storm lets up, we'll get in the canoe and get you back to camp."

Jim did not answer. It was late already. In another hour it would be dark. Then they would have trouble finding camp. A silent prayer for strength went up from his heart. They huddled miserably together.

Linda turned to Gregg. "It's all your fault," she blurted angrily. "If you hadn't been so anxious to see that stupid old eagle's nest, none of this would have happened. We'd still be back at camp."

His gaze met hers. "You were the one who told me about it – remember?"

"I know." Her voice quavered. "But I–I didn't know anything like this was going to happen." She started to cry, softly. "I didn't want to come up to this idiotic old camp in the first place. I wanted to stay back in Fairview with Dad."

The others were too cold and miserable to answer.

Cherry Adams was the one who first thought of the people back in camp. "They must have missed us by this time," she reminded them. "I'll bet Mr. Collins and Kay and the others are about frantic."

Linda turned to Gregg. "I–I just hope they're frantic enough to come out and–and look for us."

He faced her sternly. "That's enough of that kind of talk, Linda," he ordered. "If you don't stop, you'll have us all going to pieces." He took a deep breath. "The people at camp might have a terrible time finding us. We broke the rules and sneaked off without permission. We didn't even let anybody know where we were going."

Linda Penner caught her breath.

"But," Gregg continued forcefully, "we're still going to get back. If the storm ends before dark, we'll get in our canoe and go back. If it doesn't, we'll wait until it gets light in the morning. The storm won't last that long. That's for sure."

Linda's eyes widened. "You–you don't mean that w-w-we've got to stay here all night, do you?" she demanded fearfully.

Cherry broke in, her voice calm and even. "We might."

Jim closed his eyes and muffled a thin groan.

"We can't feel sorry for ourselves, Linda," the Adams girl went on. "Jim is so much worse off than we are."

Cherry took her sweater and spread it over him.

He protested strongly, "I don't need that, Cherry. I–I'm all right."

"You need it a lot worse than I do," she insisted, moving his good hand away from the sweater. "You leave that right where it is, Jim Morgan. You've got to be kept as warm as possible."

He gritted his teeth and fought against the violent shaking that had seized him and still held him in its grip.

Linda looked at Gregg and Cherry uncertainly and then down at Jim. "I–I suppose I should let him have my s-s-sweater, too," she said. "I–I'm awfully cold." She cringed under the look Gregg gave her. "I–I'm sorry." With obvious reluctance she took off her own sweater and spread it over Jim. "I didn't mean that the way it sounded."

Even though their sweaters had been wet, Linda, Cherry, and Gregg soon discovered that those garments had kept out a lot of cold. They huddled, shivering miserably.

After an hour or so the first sudden fury of the storm had dwindled, but it was still raining steadily. The cloud cover was so heavy that darkness was coming early.

Gregg sat up. "I hate to say this," he began, "but I'm afraid we're stuck here for the night." Linda gasped. "I–I can't stand it, Gregg!" she whimpered. "I just can't stand it."

He eyed her scornfully. "Well, that's just too bad, because there isn't anything we can do about it." He got to his feet. "I'm going down to see that the canoe is far enough out of the water."

When he was gone Linda turned to Cherry. "I–I'm so cold I just know that I'm going to get pneumonia, or something. I–" Her voice choked off.

Gregg Adams called out suddenly. "Our canoe! It's gone!"

CHAPTER 8

IT'S ALL YOUR FAULT!

That night was the longest that any of them had ever spent. Sometime after midnight it quit raining, but the wind came up and it seemed that the temperature skidded to freezing or below. Linda Penner and Cherry Adams huddled together, teeth chattering.

"I r-r-read something about being cold one time, Linda," Cherry mentioned.

"So did I," Linda retorted, "but it wasn't th-this cold."

"I read that if you think h-hard enough about b-being in a nice warm place you won't feel so c-c-cold."

"Did you try it?"

"It doesn't work."

There was a short silence.

They slept a little at one time or another during the night, except Jim Morgan. He closed his eyes and pretended to sleep, but that was all. His arm throbbed and his head felt light and giddy. Now and again, he broke out into a sweat, although he was as cold as the others.

Toward morning Gregg Adams got up stiffly. "If we just had some matches, we could at least build a fire and keep warm."

Jim opened his eyes weakly. "Reach in my left jeans pocket, Gregg. I think I've got a match case in there with some matches in it. At least I should have."

"How come you've got matches in your pocket?" Gregg wanted to know. "You don't smoke."

"You don't know Mr. Orlis, the man I was living with until I went to live with his son and daughter-in-law, Danny and Kay, so I could go to school. He got me a compass and a waterproof match case the first time he went to town after I came to live with them and made me promise that I'd carry them whenever I'm in the woods or lake country. I got in the habit and have had them with me ever since."

Gregg started picking up sticks from the ground. "I don't know how we're going to make this wet stuff burn," he mumbled.

Painfully Jim raised on his good elbow. "Get some small twigs off the trees, Gregg. They'll be almost dry in spite of the rain. And when you get ready to light it, strip some birch bark off the trees and light that first. It's like tinder."

Gregg did as Jim directed, and, in a few minutes, he had a good hot fire burning. Linda moved up close to it. "Oh, that feels good," she cried. "I didn't think I would ever get warm again."

Gregg looked at her without any interest. "Of course, you realize that getting warm is only one of our problems. We're still in plenty of trouble. Don't forget that. We don't have anything to eat and no way of getting back to camp."

Linda flinched. "That's right!" she exclaimed, fear coming back into her voice. "The canoe washed away, didn't it?"

* * *

At camp Kay Orlis entered the director's office wearily and dropped to a chair. "You didn't find any sign of them, Matt?" she asked.

Mr. Collins shook his head. "I sent another party out again a few minutes ago. We did find that Gregg Adams had borrowed a canoe from one of the mink farmers, but he didn't say why he wanted it or where they were going."

"Did you notify the police?"

"I just finished talking to the Mounties by radio as you came in," he replied. "They're sending planes up to help with the search."

"Would you mind trying to get Danny again?" Kay asked him. "I know he'll want to come up."

The camp director turned to the radio transmitter and flicked it on.

"I still can't understand what could have possessed them to go off this way," Kay Orlis continued. "It isn't at all like Jim. From what I've learned, the Adams boy is just as reliable."

Mr. Collins looked up momentarily. "The counselors are holding a special prayer with their campers this morning."

Kay smiled. "Thank you. It's so good to know that."

* * *

Gregg Adams picked up a piece of wood and pushed it into the fire. "You girls can get out and get some more wood," he ordered. "We can't take a chance of letting the fire go out. I just used Jim's last match."

Cherry Adams grimaced at him. "And what are you going to do while we're carrying wood?"

"I thought I'd go out and look for that canoe. There's a chance that the wind might have blown it ashore somewhere on the island."

He walked along the beach to the north end of the island, searching the water and shoreline carefully, but there was no sign of the canoe. A sick feeling came over him. If he couldn't find the canoe, they would really be in trouble. Hurriedly he retraced his steps.

Already the pangs of hunger were on him. There were plenty of fish in the lake but there was no way of getting them. He slowed his pace and looked about. There might be some berries on the island if he could find them. The saskatoons should be ripe. And there might be some blueberries around and perhaps some raspberries. If they used their heads, they ought to be able to get something to eat until the people from the camp found them.

Gregg stopped and listened intently for the sound of a plane that would indicate the search was on. But there was none. And Jim Morgan sure wasn't getting any better. A few minutes ago his face had been flushed and his eyes glazed.

At the south end of the island Gregg shaded his eyes and looked across the open expanse of water. If the canoe was out there, he wouldn't be able to get to it.

Another thought seized him – one that brought the sweat out on his forehead and set his hands trembling. If the searchers spotted the canoe, they would think the four of them had drowned. They might even quit searching! What would he and the other kids do then?

Slowly he made his way back to the place where the girls and Jim Morgan were waiting. Cherry came to meet him.

"See anything of the canoe?" she asked quietly.

He shook his head. "How's Jim?"

"His arm looks terrible, and his forehead feels awfully hot to me." She was silent for an instant or two. "And he just lies there most of the time. He hardly ever says anything."

"They just have to find us soon."

Together they walked back to where Linda Penner and Jim were waiting. The injured boy opened his eyes. Gregg saw immediately that what his sister said was true. Jim's face was flushed and dry and hot to his touch.

"See anything?" Jim asked, fighting to keep the pain out of his voice.

"Not a thing," Gregg answered calmly. "The canoe must have floated out into the big lake or ashore on some other island."

Linda Penner's cheeks went ashen.

"W-what are we going to do?" she demanded.

"What can we do?" Gregg shrugged his shoulders expressively and tried not to think of Jim. "About all we can do is wait for someone to come along and find us."

"But that might be days or–or weeks," Linda protested fearfully. "We could starve before anyone comes along."

"We're not going to starve," he patiently assured her. "The camp will have people out looking for us." He paused and glanced skyward. "Why they probably have planes out looking for us right now."

"But nobody knows where we are!" Her eyes smoldered hotly. "It's all your fault, Gregg Adams. You were the one who begged so hard to come out here and see that stupid old eagle's nest. You were the one who pleaded and pleaded until I finally agreed to bring you out and show it to you."

He eyed her coldly. "Talking like that isn't going to help us," he reminded her, "or Jim, either."

"I'm not wasting my time feeling sorry for Jim Morgan," Linda retorted. "It was his own fault that he got hurt. He had to show off by climbing that tree. Nobody asked him." Her taut voice broke angrily. "If he hadn't done such a stupid thing we'd have gotten in the canoe and been out of here before the storm hit. We wouldn't be stranded here on this island."

Gregg's mouth firmed. "That's right," he answered. "We'd probably have been right out in the middle of the big lake when that wind hit. Instead of being stranded out here, the chances are that we'd all have been drowned."

Cherry reached out and felt Jim's burning forehead. She winced involuntarily and it was a moment before she could speak. "It doesn't do any good to argue this way. Instead of fighting we ought to be praying."

"Good idea," Gregg answered. "But first I want to talk to Jim a minute." He squatted down beside his friend. "How do you feel?"

"Okay, I guess."

"Arm hurt?"

"Plenty."

"I thought it did. It sure looks bad." Gregg Adams paused. "I'm glad the weather's clear this morning. Mr. Collins'll have planes out looking for us in a little while."

Jim Morgan nodded. "Don't worry about me," he whispered. "I'll get along all right."

Cherry took out her little Bible and opened it to verse twelve in the fourteenth chapter of John. "Dad told me once that if I was ever in trouble and needed God's strength and guidance and help that I should read this verse," she recalled quietly. "It is one of God's many promises to answer our prayers."

Linda, who usually sneered at prayer, sat down and, cupping her chin in her hand, leaned forward attentively.

"Verily, verily, I say unto you, He that believeth on me, the works that I do shall he do also; and greater works than these shall he do; because I go unto my Father."

As she finished reading there was a faint humming sound in the still air.

Linda leaped to her feet excitedly. "What's that?" she demanded.

Gregg stood, too, listening intently. "It–it sounds like a plane," he ventured at last, half fearfully.

Jim raised himself on his good arm. "It is a plane!"

Gregg took a quick, deep breath. "But how are we going to signal him?" he asked helplessly. "How can we let him know that we're here?"

Even as they listened the sound of the plane began to get farther and farther away.

Gregg and Cherry Adams and Linda Penner stared disappointedly into the sky as the sound of the airplane disappeared. Jim Morgan, who was lying in silence on the ground, caught his breath sharply.

"He–he's gone, isn't he?" he asked.

Linda's thin young voice broke passionately. "He's gone! And what's more, he won't be back! They'll never find us now, Jim! They'll never find us!"

Gregg gently took her by the arm, but with a firmness he did not realize that he possessed. "Now, Linda," he ordered sternly, "that's about enough of that. You've got to get hold of yourself. Carrying on like that isn't going to do any of us any good."

She stifled a sob. "You–you just don't know how bad it is," she gasped.

"This isn't anything to be so hysterical about," Gregg continued. "Mr. Collins will get in touch with Air Rescue and the sky will be full of planes looking for us. If that plane doesn't find us, another one will."

"You're just talking that way to try to keep Cherry and me from knowing how bad it really is," she continued. "But you can't fool me. I know. I know that they'll never be able to find us."

"Now, Linda," Cherry broke in quickly. "We've been praying for God's help and guidance. We've got to trust Him."

The frightened girl was sinking her teeth into her lower lip. "I knew when I came up to this old Bible camp that something terrible was going to happen," she stammered. "I didn't want to come in the first place. I wanted to stay back in Fairview where there is something to do. But no! Dad made me come up here against my will. Now look what happened!"

Jim managed a brief grin. "Just relax and take it easy, Linda," he told her. "You're just scared again. That's the trouble with you girls. Something happens and you get all upset. Danny'll be here before long. He'll find us."

Linda whirled on him, her dark eyes blazing. "That's all I've ever heard since I've known you, Jim Morgan!" she exploded. " 'Danny will take care of it!' 'Danny knows what's best for us!' It's all because of your precious Danny Orlis that we're in this mess. If it hadn't been for him, we'd be back in Fairview having a wonderful time instead of being lost out here where we'll probably starve."

Gregg took a deep breath and expelled the air slowly. He couldn't say anything to the others right now. Linda was close enough to hysteria, and he could read the silent fright in his sister's eyes. But they were in a bad spot. Even if Mr. Collins did get Air Rescue on the job there was a lot of territory for the planes to cover, and it would be difficult for them to be seen. It might be a long time – a long, long time before they were found.

He looked down at Jim. The injured boy's face was flushed with fever, and the chances were that it would keep getting worse and worse. How long would he be able to hold out without medical attention?

Linda had started to cry again. "I–I'm hungry, Gregg! I'm practically starving."

Gregg motioned her aside with an imperative jerk of his head. When he spoke his voice was low, but authoritative. "Linda," he began guardedly, "I warned you a few minutes ago to get hold of yourself. Now do it! There's no reason for you to carry on the way you've been acting since that plane went over and didn't see us. We haven't been hurt and we're not going to be–so get hold of yourself!" As he spoke, he had taken hold of her arm again.

She jerked away, furiously. "Let go of me, Gregg Adams!" she cried. "You hurt me!"

He frowned, shaking his head in exasperation. "I almost wish you were my sister," he remarked quietly. "If you were, I'd smack you."

Her eyes met his and fought defiantly. "You wouldn't dare!"

At that moment Cherry called out. "Gregg, Jim wants to talk to you."

"I'll be right there." He started to walk away, but turned back to Linda momentarily. "Now remember what I told you. You've got to get control of yourself. This isn't any worse for you than it is for the rest of us. Just remember that."

With that he left her and went over to the place where his friend was lying. "What's on your mind?" Gregg asked.

Jim tried to hide a grimace of pain. "I just happened to think of something, Gregg," he told his friend. "Once when we were on the Angle, a couple of hunters were lost for two or three days. I remember

Mr. Orlis saying that if they had just built a good smudge fire with plenty of smoke, they could have drawn the searchers right to them."

Gregg's eyes lighted. "That's it!" he exclaimed. "I don't know why we didn't think of that before. Smoke would be easy to see – especially from the air." He turned to the girls. "I'm going to get some more wood. While I'm gone, get some green leaves and grass. We're going to build the biggest, smokiest fire!"

Linda pouted. "I don't know whether I care to get any leaves and grass or not after the way you've been treating me since we've been stranded here."

"Okay," Gregg replied indifferently. "If you want to stay out here, don't get any green stuff for the fire. It's okay with me."

Her eyes blazed angrily, but she turned quickly to the task of gathering leaves and grass. In a few minutes the fire was putting out a great column of choking gray smoke.

Cherry turned uncertainly to her brother. "Gregg."

He did not answer her immediately. "Gregg," she repeated, "how–how long do you suppose it's going to be before a plane sees the smoke!"

His forehead rumpled thoughtfully. "That's hard to say," he answered. "A plane may fly over in the next five minutes, or it may be several hours. The important thing, though, is for us to be sure and have that smoke rising strongly enough when the planes are in the air that they'll be sure and see it."

"Do you think they'll see it b-b-before dark," she asked, "so we won't have to spend another night out here?"

"We'll have to pray that they will."

The smile of relief that had come to Linda's face the instant she thought rescue would be momentary gave way to wild, unreasoning fright. "I don't think I can stand it another night here," she announced almost hysterically. "There may be b-b-bears on this island and everything."

Nobody answered her.

In a few minutes Cherry called Linda down by the lake with her. "Have you felt Jim's forehead lately?" she asked.

The Penner girl shook her head.

"His fever's getting higher all the time. I don't know what we'll do if we aren't able to get medicine for him soon. He's apt to get pneumonia and–and–" Her voice trailed away significantly.

Linda glanced back at the place where Jim was lying. "His face is flushed, isn't it?" she admitted.

"I felt his forehead just a minute ago and he's burning up," Cherry declared. "I'm afraid he's awful sick, Linda."

The other girl's lower lip quivered. "I–I thought perhaps he was getting along," she said. "He hasn't done much except groan a little."

"That's because he doesn't want to upset the rest of us any more than we're upset already," Cherry explained. For a brief instant Linda eyed her companion honestly. "I–I don't want to go to pieces the way I've been doing, Cherry," she confessed, "honestly I don't. But I just can't help it. I–I'm scared. I'm awful scared!"

Cherry nodded understandingly. "I'll let you in on a secret, Linda. I'm scared, too."

CHAPTER 9

CAN'T YOU MAKE HIM UNDERSTAND?

Back at the Bible camp on the mainland Kay Orlis handed the two-way radio mike back to the operator. "I'm so glad we were able to get hold of Danny," she smiled. "I know I'll feel better when he gets here."

The camp director nodded. "I can understand that," Matt Collins remarked. "He's coming right up, isn't he?"

"He sounded as though he'll be here quite early tomorrow morning. He said he wanted to get in touch with Mr. Penner so he can come up with him, too." Once more Matt nodded. "Good idea," he replied. "I was just going to ask for Mr. Penner's information so I could notify him. I just got in touch with the Adams kids' parents. They'll be here some time tomorrow."

Kay's young face was ashen with concern. "Do–do you think the kids are all right?"

The camp director frowned. "I don't know why they don't follow regulations about staying on the campgrounds. It's things like this that cause trouble, Kay – always."

* * *

Danny Orlis left the home of the ham radio operator where he had been summoned to talk to Kay and went directly to the dairy where Henry Penner worked.

The dairy manager picked up his hat and started for the door. "I think I know where Henry will be about this time of day," he informed him. "I'll take a relief driver out to take over for him and bring him directly to the airport. He ought to be there by the time you're ready to take off."

True to his word, by the time Danny had the plane filled with gas and ready to take off, Henry was there. Linda's dad leaped from his employer's car and came running across the apron to the place where the Cessna 180 was sitting.

"Danny!" he cried, "where's Linda? What has happened to her?"

"We don't know that anything has happened to her, Henry," young Orlis replied calmly. "There isn't anything to get so alarmed about."

Henry was trembling violently. "What happened to her?" he demanded. "Tell me!"

"All I really know is what I told Mr. Brown. Linda

and some of the kids wandered away from camp and they haven't been able to locate them."

"Wandered away?" Henry's voice rose and broke. "What's the matter with those people up there? Can't they keep track of a few children? If something has happened to Linda, I–I'll hold them responsible! That's what I'll do!"

Danny's voice was calm and reassuring. "Now, Henry, get hold of yourself."

Henry climbed into the plane and fastened his seat belt with trembling fingers. "I should never have let her go up to that camp anyway," he blurted. "I ought to have let her stay at home the way she wanted to. Then I'd have her. She'd be right here with me!"

Danny started the engine and let it turn over slowly to warm up. "Now, Henry," he reminded him, "we don't know that anything has happened to the kids. They went out in a canoe and haven't come back. There are a lot of things that could have delayed them. They could have lost a paddle. They could have gone ashore somewhere and the canoe could have drifted away from them. Don't be so upset until we actually find out what the situation is."

Henry's face tightened. "How long has it been since they've been seen?" he asked.

Danny's eyes clouded. "Some time yesterday afternoon."

* * *

On the other side of the lake from the Bible camp, Gregg Adams threw another armload of leaves and grass on the fire. Acrid gray smoke swirled upward.

"That isn't doing any good!" Linda Penner's voice bordered on hysteria. "That isn't doing a bit of good!"

Gregg started to reply sharply, but something out in the lake caught his eye. "Look!" he cried, pointing a trembling finger.

Gleefully Cherry cried out, "A canoe!"

Gregg and Cherry Adams stared across the choppy water, stricken dumb momentarily. The boy moistened his lips with the tip of his tongue and swallowed hard. A sudden weakness drained the strength from his legs. Cherry, too, was struck motionless.

Linda leaped to her feet excitedly. "It is a canoe!" she cried. "And–and they're heading right toward us!" She shouted into the wind. "Yoo-hoo! Yoo-hoo! Over here!" As she shouted she dashed forward, almost tripping over a rock.

Jim Morgan laughed in spite of his pain. "Hey, Linda!" he called out, "take it easy or you'll scare 'em away!"

But she did not even hear him. She dashed down to the water's edge, yelling and waving her arms in desperation. Cherry and Gregg Adams were right behind her. Cherry pulled up slowly.

"Gregg," she whispered fearfully, "they–they're Indians!"

He stopped and grinned at her. "Who else would you expect out here?" he asked. "We're in Indian territory. The chances are that we're on an Indian reservation right now."

Realization of the identity of their visitors came slowly to Linda. When she did see them clearly, she stopped short and held out her hand. "Gregg," she gasped. "Gregg."

He came up beside her. "What's the matter?" he asked.

"Gregg, do–do you see who's out there?"

He laughed heartily. "I sure do. And I'm mighty glad to see them. I don't care who they are!"

"But, Gregg," she protested, "they–they're Indians!"

"Don't let that get you all shaken up," he answered. "There are a lot more Indians out here than there are whites!"

Linda's voice was trembling. "Gregg," she faltered, "you stay right close to me. You–you won't go away and l-leave me, will you, Gregg?"

"These Indians aren't going to hurt us."

She shuddered. "But just look at them. T-t-they're so–so dark."

Gregg turned to her. "That's just about enough, Linda," he commanded sternly. "It doesn't make any difference if those people are dark or light. They've seen our smoke signal and they're coming to help us. Just remember that."

She sneered at him, defiantly. "Don't use that tone of voice with me," she snapped back. "I'll have you know that I'm not used to being talked to that way."

"If you don't treat these people as friends and show that you appreciate the fact that they've come to help us, you'll have to answer to me," he warned her darkly. "That's a promise."

She snorted. However, as the long, slender canoe moved closer to shore, she scooted closer and closer to Gregg, "I–I'm sorry, Gregg." Her voice was a whisper. "Don't go away and leave me, Gregg – not even for a minute."

A moment or two later the canoe bearing the Indian man and his wife came ashore almost at their feet. The slender, dark-skinned man appeared to be forty or forty-five years old. His shy, attractive wife was probably a few years younger. She sat in the prow, a paddle in her hand. For a moment or two they sat there, the canoe keel grating on the sand. Their faces were expressionless as they looked from Gregg to Cherry to Linda and back again.

Gregg grinned in greeting. "Hello."

There was no answer.

"Hey, are we glad to see you!" he continued.

The Indian spoke to him rapidly in a tongue the auburn-haired boy had never heard before.

Gregg's mouth sagged open. "Don't you speak English?" Gregg asked.

The man spoke again in deep, guttural tones.

Gregg tried again. "Speak English?"

The Indian broke off talking and a blank look gleamed in his eyes.

Cherry touched her brother on the arm. "Gregg, I don't believe either one of them understands a single word of English."

For answer the Indian man rose and stepped ashore. He pointed to the fire and, with an exaggerated motion, gestured skyward.

"They saw our smoke." Gregg spoke numbly. "That must have been what brought them over here."

The Indian woman had remained motionless in the canoe until she spied Jim. She half turned, then, and spoke softly to her husband. He replied and she got out of the canoe and went half running up the beach to the place where Jim was lying. She knelt beside him, her deft, tender touch cool to his fevered arm.

Gregg and the girls followed a few steps behind the Indian couple.

Jim smiled away the pain. "Boy, I sure am glad to see you," he greeted her. "To tell you the truth, I was beginning to wonder if we were going to have to stay out here for a month or two."

Gregg caught the injured boy's eye. "They don't understand any English, " he said softly.

A blank look of unbelief came to his eyes. "You mean they don't understand a thing?"

"They don't know a single word of English," Gregg went on. "We didn't even get any response when I spoke to them."

Concern flickered in Jim's eyes. "That's tough." He expelled his breath with a rush. "Think we can make them understand that we want to go over to camp?"

Gregg shrugged. "We don't even know if they're aware that there is such a thing as the camp."

Linda gasped.

Jim glanced in her direction. "Now what's the matter with you?" he asked.

She stifled a sob. "We're in just as big a mess as we've always been," she said, her voice breaking. "We're never going to get out of here."

All the while they had been talking, the Indian woman had continued to expertly examine Jim Morgan's arm. Every now and then she spoke to her husband in low, murmuring tones. After a moment he got to his feet and went to the canoe. He returned with two straight, smooth sticks twelve to fourteen inches long.

She turned to Linda and motioned. The girl paled and shrank away. The woman motioned again.

Cherry was the first to understand what she meant. "She just wants to borrow your scarf, Linda," she explained.

The Indian woman took it and, tearing it in two, bound the splints firmly on either side of Jim Morgan's injured arm.

The kids had not even noticed that the Indian man had gone until he came back several minutes later with a bird he had shot.

Gregg touched Jim's thigh. "Look at that, would you?" he exclaimed gleefully. "I think we're going to eat."

The woman went back to her canoe, got a small kettle, and filled it half full of water. While she was doing that her husband built a small fire.

Cherry turned to Linda and smiled. "Know something?" she echoed. "I think Gregg's right for once. It does look as though we're going to eat."

Before they ate, they bowed their heads and prayed. Gregg saw that the Indians eyed them curiously and talked between themselves. "Doesn't that hurt, Cherry?" he asked her. "These people don't even know what it is to ask God's blessing on their food."

"I knew there were people like that in Africa and Borneo and places like that, but not right here in Canada," she replied.

When they had finished eating, the Indian couple motioned for them to come to the canoe.

Linda's eyes widened in terror. "W-w-what do they want?" she asked.

"It looks to me as though they want us to get in the canoe with them and go somewhere," Gregg replied.

Her face paled. "We–we aren't going to do it, are we?" she asked. "We're not going to go with these–these savages, are we, Gregg?" Her voice broke tearfully.

* * *

Danny Orlis had only been able to go part way to the Bible camp the same evening they left Fairview. They were up at four o'clock the next morning and shortly after eight touched down at the landing strip near the camp. Kay Orlis and Matt Collins hurried out to the plane.

"Have you heard anything yet?" Henry Penner demanded, crawling out of the aircraft. "Do you know where Linda is?"

The camp superintendent's face was taut and drawn, and his eyes dark with sleeplessness. "The planes are out now," he replied, "but we haven't had any report yet."

Kay broke in quickly. "We were expecting them to start reporting about the time we saw you. Maybe we'll have word when we get back."

Henry wiped his hand across his sweating forehead. "I should have kept Linda with me this summer," he said to no one in particular. "That's what she wanted. She didn't want to come up here and–" His voice broke off uncertainly. "I don't mean to blame you or anyone else for what happened. I know it wasn't your fault. You were taking the best care of her that you could." He paused and looked about. "But to come to a desolate place like this! I should have known better than to let her come."

Neither Danny nor Kay answered him.

Collins turned to the youthful pilot. "Are you going to join the search, Danny?" he asked.

"Just as soon as I can fill with gas."

"That's fine," Matt put in, "but I don't have to warn you not to go out too far, Danny. You'll be flying with wheels, remember?"

As soon as the Cessna was filled with gas, Danny and Mr. Penner got into the plane, took off, and circled at a level not too far above the treetops. Henry lifted his voice above the even, rhythmic throb of the motor.

"What are we looking for?" he asked.

"Smoke, a sign of the kids on a beach somewhere, or maybe a canoe," Danny told him.

Henry Penner bowed his head and prayed silently. After he had finished, Danny Orlis glanced over at him.

"You know, Henry," he said, "it's during times like these that the Lord is very close to us. All we have to do is to put our trust in Him and He will take care of us and give us the strength and courage we need."

The concerned father nodded understandingly. For several minutes they flew in silence. Then Henry Penner grasped Danny's arm.

"Dan!" he cried. "Look down there!"

Danny banked sharply. "What did you think you saw?"

"I–I'm not sure." His voice was trembling so he could scarcely speak. "I–I don't know for sure, but I thought I saw something flash in the sun. Something like a–a canoe."

Danny Orlis brought the plane about. It was two or three minutes before he could sight the thing that had caught his passenger's attention. As he did so his heart faltered. It was a canoe, all right! Turned upside down and washed ashore on a desolate stretch of beach!

CHAPTER 10

LOST IN THE MIDDLE OF NOWHERE

Danny Orlis dipped low over the beach, twin lights of fear flaming in his widening eyes.

"Danny!" Henry Penner's tight voice tremored. "Danny! The canoe is capsized!"

The young pilot put down the fear that tugged at his own heart. His voice was calm enough, but his hand trembled as he switched on the radio and contacted the camp director.

"See anything of the kids?" Matt Collins asked.

"Not yet. All we see is an overturned canoe washed up on the beach."

The camp director gasped.

"We'll circle the area until a floatplane arrives."

Henry sat in silence, his lips working wordlessly. The color had gone out of his cheeks and his lips were blue and lifeless.

There must have been another plane not far away, for Danny and Henry had only been circling for ten minutes or so when a floatplane came winging in. Danny tightened his circle banking over the canoe until the other pilot waggled his wings as a signal that he had spotted it.

For the first time Henry took his eyes off the canoe below them. He turned to Danny, despair clouding his face. "What are we going to do now, Danny?" he asked miserably.

"We'll go back, get into a floatplane, and come out here just as quickly as we can."

"Do–do you think there's any hope?" Henry managed.

"Of course there is," Danny retorted evenly. "There's a good chance that the kids aren't even hurt. The canoe could have a hole bashed in it or something, or maybe it drifted away from them."

"Or–" The other man's voice choked. "Or, they could have tried to make it back to camp before the storm hit and got caught out in the wind. If that happened, they–they're–"

The Cessna 180 touched down smoothly.

"Like I told you, Henry, I don't know this other boy, but I do know Jim Morgan. And I know how well Dad taught him about the lakes and storms. Jim wouldn't take a chance. You can be sure of that."

"I wish I could be just as sure that Linda didn't," Henry said.

* * *

Gregg Adams looked down at his sister Cherry and Jim Morgan with a questioning frown. The Indian man gestured again.

"He wants us to go with them," Gregg explained. "What do you think?"

Before anyone else could speak Linda Penner broke in hurriedly. "They can't go away and leave us! If they do, we won't have anything to eat. We–we'll starve!"

Gregg snapped a twig from a nearby branch and began to strip off the bark thoughtfully. "If we go with them," he suggested, "we may miss the search party."

Cherry was looking down at Jim. "But the searchers might be several days in finding us," she reminded him. "And the Indian woman does act as though she knows how to take care of Jim – at least a lot better than we do."

"Make them stay here!" Linda's voice rose. "Just make them stay with us until the planes find us. That won't be more than a few days."

Gregg threw the twig away. "And just how do you figure on making them stay here, Linda?" he asked quietly. "We can't talk to them. If we could, we could ask them to take us over to the camp. As kind as they are, I'm sure they would do that."

Jim reached up with his good hand and pulled at Gregg's pants leg. "Hey, I've got an idea," he broke in.

"I'm glad somebody has."

"Did you ever try to see if you could make them understand that we came from the Bible camp and that we want to go back over there?" he asked.

"I don't know," Gregg hesitated doubtfully. "I haven' t had much success so far in getting things across to them, but I can try."

He went over to the place where the Indian man was standing and made a crude drawing of the lake in the sand. Then he pointed to the canoe and the place on the rough sketch where the camp was located. Blankly the Indian shook his head. Gregg went through the motions again, but without success.

"It's no use, Gregg," Cherry put in.

He looked up at his younger sister. "What can we do, except to go along with them?"

Linda cried a little when she learned what they were going to do, but when the time came to leave, she got into the canoe with the rest of them.

The Indian canoe was larger than average, but it was scarcely made for six and rode low in the water. Jim Morgan reached out and touched the surface of the water with his fingers.

"We're riding low," he reminded them. "I'm sure glad it's a calm day."

Gregg picked up an extra paddle and, squatting amidships, began to help out. The Indian man nodded and grunted approvingly. The Indian couple went across a narrow stretch of water, cut around an island, and headed down a thin, twisting stream.

Jim's face grew serious. "Know something, Gregg? We're sure going to be a powerful long way from that Bible camp. It's not going to make it any easier for anyone to find us."

Gregg did not miss a stroke with his paddle, but the uneasiness within him grew. The smart thing would have been to have stayed on the island where they had been stranded. He knew that. Everything he had ever read about anyone getting lost had hammered at that advice. But this was different. Jim was hurt and his fever was crawling higher and higher. The Indian woman knew how to take care of him. Going along was the only thing they could do. Each stroke of the paddle was a prayer for guidance and strength for all of them, and especially for Jim.

They had been gone from the island an hour or so when they heard the sound of a plane in the distance.

Linda's head snapped up as she began to search the sky excitedly. "Somebody's coming!" she cried. "Maybe they're going to find us after all!"

Jim listened intently, fighting against the nausea that swept over him. "That sounds like a Cessna 180," he added.

"That's what Danny flies, isn't it?" Linda's voice betrayed her excitement and concern. "Do you suppose that could be Danny?"

"It could be." Gregg tried to hide the despair in his voice. "But whoever it is isn't coming any closer to us."

At last Cherry spoke up. "You know, that plane sounds to me as though it must be in the area where we just were."

Linda broke into a sob. "Oh, no! "

* * *

The camp superintendent had a floatplane waiting for Danny and Mr. Penner, and in a matter of minutes they were back at the place where the canoe had been found. The first pilot to arrive had already pulled the canoe up on shore and was examining it carefully. He glanced over his shoulder as Danny and his companions came up.

"Hi."

Henry Penner squatted down beside him, his face a mask of dread. "What do you think?" he asked weakly.

The pilot pursed his lips. "There's some gear here that must have come out of the canoe, a life belt and a paddle. So that means it didn't overturn out in the lake. This stuff spilled out after the canoe washed ashore."

Danny noted the tear in the aluminum skin. "And this was done on the rocks," he added. "That's another sign that it floated in here right side up." His smile widened. "I'm confident now that the kids got ashore alive."

* * *

It was late that night when the Indian couple finally brought the kids to their destination, a little clearing along a lake where there were several tents and a small log hut. Three or four children and two older Indians came down to the beach curiously and gathered about.

Gregg Adams turned to his sister. "I thought maybe there would be someone here who could speak English, but I don't believe there is," he told her.

The Indian man motioned them toward the biggest tent. "What are they going to do to us?" Linda Penner wanted to know.

The tent to which the Indian took them was about twelve feet long and with a bark-covered room half that size tacked on one end.

Gregg looked about. "Cherry," he said, "you and Linda can sleep in the tent. Jim and I will sleep out here in this bark hut."

A moment or two later the Indians brought them portions of thick stew. Gregg tasted it.

"Wow, is this ever great!"

The following morning everyone else was up and dressed by the time Jim Morgan awoke. He rolled over on his side and opened one eye. Gregg was sitting, cross-legged, nearby.

"You're looking better, Jim," his friend told him. "How're you feeling?"

"I feel a lot better than I did yesterday. I don't know what that Indian woman gave me, but it sure went to work on that fever."

"I've heard about some of their old family remedies," Gregg answered. "They must have a pretty good line of medicines, considering the fact that they mostly use herbs and things like that." He looked down at Jim's arm. "How's the old wing today?"

The injured boy grimaced. "It still hurts like every-thing, but I don't think it's swollen quite as bad as it was. At least it doesn't feel that way."

They heard a chipmunk chattering brazenly at them from a nearby poplar.

"Have you ever seen any people as friendly as this Indian family?" Gregg asked at last.

There was a short silence. "I lay awake for a long while last night just thinking about them," Jim admitted. "And do you realize that we haven't even been able to talk to them? We haven't been able to make them understand a single word we've said. Still, they've taken us in and have taken care of us as though we were their very own."

"It sure makes you feel grateful and humble, doesn't it? We'd be in an awful mess if it hadn't been for them."

Jim Morgan sat up and leaned against the crude bark wall of the little hut in which they had been sleeping. "There's another thing that has grabbed me in a way that it never has before. The very fact that no one here can speak English has really bothered me. Somehow, we always think of countries across the ocean or down in South America when we think of people speaking different languages. But that isn't it at all. We have them living right here in Canada, and, I suppose, back in the States, too."

An Indian boy came to the door of the hut and peeked in, grinning warmly. Gregg and Jim smiled their greeting to him, and in an instant he had run to play.

Jim continued. "And the thing that is so pitiful is that these people are lost – absolutely and forever lost unless someone brings them the gospel." He took a long breath. "And who is there to tell them of Christ?"

"Aren't there some missionaries working up here, Jim?"

"Quite a few of them," Jim replied, "but there aren't nearly enough, and there isn't nearly enough money to build mission stations, either."

"I'd always thought that being a missionary was a real waste of a person 's life until we were taken in by this family. It sure looks different when you get to know the people and to realize what they are like and how badly they need the gospel."

The boys had breakfast together and sauntered down toward the lake.

"It sure is good to have you on your feet, Jim," Gregg told him.

"You can say that again."

The Adams boy picked up a stone and sent it skittering across the placid water. "How long do you suppose we'll be up here before someone picks us up?" he asked.

Jim leaned against a tree and touched his injured arm thoughtfully. "I wish I knew. It shouldn't be too long now. They'll keep looking for us until they find us – I hope."

"I went walking along the shore yesterday and found a little cabin a mile or so away. It really gave me a lift to see it. I figured that sooner or later whoever owns it is going to show up."

Jim laughed. "You probably found an old trapping cabin."

"I don't care what it is, just as long as somebody comes up to live in it."

"That's just the trouble," he continued. "If it's an old trapping cabin it won't be used until trapping season."

The light went out of Gregg's eyes.

It was late the following afternoon when a floatplane came directly over the little clearing. It came winging out of the south and made a lazy semicircle almost directly over them.

Linda, who had been discouraged and was lying in the tent, heard the approaching whine of the engine. She sat up straight, listening. A plane! A plane! She scrambled outside and looked skyward, hope and fear squeezing at her lungs. At first her eyes could not pick up the silver craft, and a nameless dread swept over her.

For a brief, tantalizing moment it appeared as though the plane had seen them. The pilot banked and started to come about. Then he straightened and put the light craft into a long glide. She waited in dismay until it disappeared behind the trees.

Linda began to sob.

CHAPTER 11

CLUTCHING AT A STRAW

Danny Orlis, the two Mounties, Captain Vogel and Constable Reams, and the superintendent of the Bible camp got together that night after the searchers came staggering in.

Captain Vogel took his phone from his pocket and wrote: "Another day and we haven't seen a sign of those kids. I don't see how they could have disappeared so quickly." He put the phone away. "Of course, we've only begun to check out the islands in that area. We may turn up something encouraging yet."

Danny turned from the map he had been studying. "The remains of that fire we found at the other end of the island where we located the canoe was the most hopeful sign we've had as far as I'm concerned," Danny put in. "In my own mind, I'm convinced that the kids built that fire."

Captain Vogel pursed his lips. "That could be, but

it could have been a lot of other people, too. You soon learn in this business not to take anything for granted."

Constable Reams joined in. "I feel the same as Orlis does about that fire. It wouldn't have been made for a shore lunch by fishermen. They would never have carried all their gear so far from the water."

Danny nodded. "There's another thing about that fire," he continued. "I don't think it was even built to cook on. There were no stones around it. It was the sort of a fire someone would make to dry out and get warm – something the kids would have had to do if they were caught out in that storm."

Captain Vogel was still not convinced. "I know all that," he assured them, "but if the kids built the fire, what happened to them? If they were on that island and built that fire, they'd still be there."

The young Mountie's eyes gleamed. "That puzzles me, too," the constable agreed. "But there may be a very logical answer to that."

"What do you mean?"

"I was born and raised in this country," he went on. "It is a desolate place, but there are times when there's a lot more traffic on the lake than you would think. Someone might have come along and taken them away."

Vogel was not impressed. "Anyone who would have found them would have brought them back to the camp." He shook his head. "No, Reams, I can't buy that. I think something else happened to them."

"If someone who could speak English found them, what you say is true. But there are a lot of Indians up here who don't speak English. If one of those men came along, the kids wouldn't be able to tell them who they were or where they wanted to go. In a case like that, the Indian or Indians might just take them along with them."

Captain Vogel's forehead knotted. "Now, that's something that had never occurred to me," he confessed. "We'll check out every Indian camp and cabin in the area, starting the first thing in the morning." He got to his feet, his weariness showing in every movement of his big frame. "It means that our job is going to be a much bigger one than we had anticipated. But at least we've got something to work on."

Danny turned to him. "You won't stop the other search, will you?" he asked.

"Oh, no, this just means that we've got twice as much to do."

* * *

The following morning when Gregg Adams and Jim Morgan awakened, they became more discouraged than ever. A heavy overcast blotted out the sun and great drops of water splashed on the canvas. Jim raised himself on one elbow and looked out at the gray, dripping sky.

"It doesn't look as though there'll be anyone around looking for us today," he sighed, fighting discouragement in his voice.

"They won't be able to fly," Gregg answered. "That's for sure." He rolled over on his side. "Do you realize how long it's been that we've been here, Jim? And we're no closer to getting out than we were the first day that we came."

Jim nodded. "Your parents and Linda's dad and Danny and Kay are probably all about sick with worry." He sat up again. "Know something, Gregg? It was pretty stupid for us to break the rules and leave camp the way we did."

"Say that again."

"And it was even more stupid for me to climb that tree to get a picture of that eagle's nest. It's a wonder I wasn't killed."

"It's when we do things like we did that we get into all sorts of trouble," Gregg went on. "We should know by this time that rules at school, or camp, or in our homes are only to help us and to keep us out of trouble."

Jim managed a sheepish little grin. "I can tell you one thing. If we ever get back, I'll bet there are four of us who'll never break camp regulations again."

The boys left the little bark hut together. Gregg directed his attention up at the clouds that seemed to be but a scant few yards above the treetops. It had stopped raining, but water was dripping everywhere.

"I've tried to hide it as much as I could, Jim," his friend confided at last, "but I've been awfully discouraged the past two or three days. I thought sure that Air Rescue or somebody would have come along and found us by this time."

"They've flown over us a number of times, but the trouble is that we can't signal them because we're here at an Indian camp. If they were to see a smoke signal, they would just think the Indians were smoking fish or moose meat."

"I suppose you're right," Gregg told him. "And with your arm the way it is and us not having a canoe or anything, we don't have much of a chance of getting away."

They were still standing there talking when they caught a glimpse of a canoe rounding the point of an island a couple of miles away.

"Jim, do you see what I see?" Gregg pointed, trembling.

"A canoe!" Jim cried. "Somebody's coming, at last!"

Gregg glanced about, quickly. "I don't think the girls have seen it," he said, keeping his voice low. "Maybe we shouldn't let them know about it – just in case it doesn't pan out."

Jim Morgan started forward. "Good idea. It'd just make them feel worse than ever – especially Linda."

They sauntered, with exaggerated carelessness, down to the water's edge.

Gregg's young body was quivering with excitement. "I believe they're headed this way," he whispered tensely.

True enough. The canoe was coming in their direction. It was moving very slowly, but it was moving. There was no doubt of that.

Perspiration came out on Jim Morgan's forehead and, for an instant or two at least, the dull ache in his arm disappeared. "If there was only some way to signal them!"

Gregg caught his breath. "We could take a canoe and go out to meet them! That would be the surest way."

Jim glanced around, wildly. "There's no way to go. The canoes are all out!" Briefly despair overwhelmed him. "Maybe that's one of the Indians out there," he said numbly.

Gregg shook his head. "It can't be. They don't have canoes like that one."

The two boys stood there, breathlessly, watching the canoe.

"That could be another Indian who doesn't speak English, though," Gregg put in. "And if it is, it won't do us any good."

For several minutes neither spoke.

"Whoever it is, they don't seem to be moving this way very fast. I wonder if they're moving at all."

"I see now!" Jim exclaimed. "They're fishing! That's why they aren't moving in this direction any faster than they are."

Gregg grasped the injured boy's good arm. "Jim!" he cried. "I know who those guys are now! You remember that plane that went so low over us a couple of days ago. I'll bet it flew in here with those guys so they could fish."

Jim's eyes gleamed with excitement. "You're right!"

he agreed. "That plane did look as though it went down behind the trees, come to think of it. Remember how we watched it, and it didn't come up again."

"That means those men speak English!" Gregg's grip tightened on his friend's arm. "They're probably white men who came in to fish."

Jim did not answer him. He was too busy praying.

All too slowly the canoe made its way along the island. The distance between it and the Indian camp shortened.

"Think we can signal them yet?" Jim asked finally.

Gregg shook his head. "Not until they get a little closer. They'd never see us from here."

"What if they don't get any closer?" Jim's lips scarcely formed the words.

Gregg Adams' face went ashen. "We'll have to pray that they do!" he gasped.

CHAPTER 12

IS THIS MY CALL FOR LIFE?

While Gregg Adams and Jim Morgan watched breathlessly, the canoe made its way out to a rocky shoal half a mile from the Indian camp. Gregg waved desperately and shouted. The men in the canoe waved back.

"They've seen us!" Gregg shouted loudly. "They've seen us!"

One minute dragged by, and then another. At last the canoe turned and headed diagonally across the narrow stretch of water toward the mainland where the camp was located. But they were not coming to the camp. They were heading up the lake in the direction the plane had disappeared.

The boys both noticed it about the same time. Jim's dismay sapped his strength.

"They're going on, Gregg," he said miserably. "They're not coming here after all!"

Wearily Gregg sank to the ground. "It's no use, Jim. We can't attract their attention. We're never going to get out of here!"

"Don't talk that way. You sound like Linda. We've got to trust in the Lord."

"I know that," Gregg replied, "but it's sure hard when day after day goes by and nobody comes for us. We've been praying and praying that God will provide some way for us to get back to the Bible camp, Jim, but it doesn't seem to do any good. We're still stuck out here."

A drop of rain hit Jim in the face. He touched the wet spot on the side of his nose and looked up. "We'd better be getting back to the tent. It's going to be raining in a couple of minutes."

Gregg Adams took half a step toward the bark and canvas shelter before stopping suddenly. "Jim!" New hope tinged his voice. "I know where those fishermen are going to be in about two minutes after it starts to rain."

His friend eyed him in amazement. "Are you nuts?" Jim demanded. "They'll be right out there in the lake, getting wet – but that won't do us a bit of good."

"That's what you think. Look at them!" He pointed out at the fishermen. "They've headed in the general direction of that trapper's cabin. As soon as it starts to rain, they'll pull in their lines, head for shore, and take shelter in that hut."

Excitement gleamed in Jim's eyes. "I think you may have something, at that."

By this time rain was dimpling the placid lake and the wind was beginning to rustle in the trees.

"The wind's coming up, too," Gregg continued. "That's going to help drive them ashore." He started up the beach on the run. "When those guys get there, I'm going to be right there waiting for them. I'll be back as soon as I can."

Jim watched in tense silence as his red-haired friend went dashing toward the trapper's cabin. A prayer welled within his heart.

As though Gregg's move for the trapper's cabin was the signal, the clouds seemed to split, and torrents of water slanted down. At the same time the wind gathered strength, and, with a great rushing noise, lashed the lake to a frenzy and drove the rain before it.

But Gregg did not slacken his pace. The first downpour soaked him to the skin, and the wind drove the cold deeply into his bones. But there was a prayer of hope and thanksgiving in every step. "Oh, God," he prayed in desperation, "help me to get there in time! Help me to get to them before they leave!"

Strange, but he seemed to know, instinctively, that the men were there. He had covered half the distance to the old trapper's cabin when the rain began to slacken. Only slightly at first, he scarcely noticed the change. But another five minutes and the rain had all but stopped.

Frenzy seized him! The breath seared his lungs as he fought his way forward. He had to get to them! And yet, in his burning anxiety it seemed that he was scarcely running at all. Harder and harder he pushed himself. The wind died down as suddenly as it came up. The rain stopped, and all was quiet again.

Another three hundred yards – two hundred – now he was around the last sharp bend and could see the cabin. There was the canoe! The men were just getting back into it!

"Hello!" he cried out desperately.

The men stopped and stared at him in astonishment. Gregg didn't speak again until he staggered up to them. Even then, it was a moment or two before he could get his breath enough to say anything.

One of the men ran over and grasped him by the shoulders. "What's the matter, boy?" he demanded. "What's wrong?"

At last he found voice. "I–I was afraid you'd be gone before I–I got here."

"Who are you?"

"I'll bet this is one of those kids who's lost, Mickey," the other fisherman suggested. "You know, we heard about them on the radio coming in the other night."

"T-t-that's right," Gregg agreed. Breathing heavily, he gasped out the story.

The one called Mickey turned to his fishing companion. "I'll tell you what. You go over with the kid and see that the others are all right. I'll go back to the plane and radio in that we've found them."

It didn't seem true. It couldn't be true. Yet it was! They had help at last!

"Thank You, God!" He spoke with such fervor that both men turned and stared at him. "Thank You for sending these men to help us!"

* * *

All that day the clouds and wind and rain made it impossible for the planes to come and pick up the kids, but the following morning the weather cleared slightly, and two float planes flew in to get Jim Morgan and his companions. Danny Orlis flew one of them. He had brought a doctor as his passenger to examine Jim. For a few minutes everyone was laughing and talking at once.

Then, while the doctor was completing his examination, Danny turned to Linda Penner. "Your dad's over at camp, Linda," he told her. "He's certainly anxious to see you."

Her lower lip curled. "If he had just let me stay home in Fairview with him this summer the way I wanted to, this wouldn't have happened," she moaned. "I don't see why I had to come up to this stupid old camp, anyway."

Danny let it pass.

Cherry Adams stood close by while the doctor examined Jim Morgan's arm and took his temperature.

"How is he, Doctor?" Her young voice tremored slightly.

"He seems to be getting along splendidly. We're going to have to take an X- ray of his arm to see just how the bone is set, but even that seems to be all right. I can't feel any bumps or ridges that would indicate it hadn't been properly lined up."

Cherry sighed her relief.

Jim grinned self-consciously as Danny came over and stood beside Gregg's sister. "I knew everything was all right," Jim told them. "I felt fine after that Indian woman started taking care of me. I don't know what sort of medicine she gave me, but it sure did help get rid of that fever."

"There's something else I'm sure you didn't know, Jim," Danny put in. "The tribe this family belongs to is the one that Roxie was planning on working with before the Lord called her home."

Jim's young face was serious. "It sort of makes me feel as though I ought to come out here as a missionary myself. These people need the gospel so much."

"Every person who hasn't heard that Christ is the only Savior needs the gospel desperately, Jim," Danny Orlis reminded him.

* * *

That afternoon Danny flew Jim down to the nearest hospital to have his arm X-rayed. The picture confirmed the doctor's first diagnosis.

"In fact," the doctor told them, "I must say that the condition of this arm is remarkable. It was a good, clean break, and apparently the bones did not get out of line. It's in place perfectly. I don't mind telling you that I find it difficult to understand."

"An Indian woman put splints on it for me," Jim told him.

"She must have done that before you were moved very far, young man." There was a short silence. "You can be very thankful that she came along. If you had gone this long without having that arm held firmly in place you'd be in for some real trouble. We would undoubtedly have to put you in the hospital and break it over so it could be reset."

The following morning Danny Orlis took the first load back to Fairview. The next day he came back for Jim Morgan and Linda Penner.

Jim got into the plane beside Danny and leaned back in the seat. " I'm sure glad to be heading back to Fairview. For a long while I didn't know whether we would ever get back there or not."

Linda snorted. "It was all your fault, I say. If you hadn't been showing off in front of that snippy Cherry Adams, you wouldn't have gotten hurt, and we would have gotten back to camp before that storm broke!"

Jim colored deeply.

Danny's gaze met his. "Now what's this about Cherry Adams?" he asked.

Jim frowned. "Nothing," he mumbled. "Nothing at all."

"You were showing off for her, Jim Morgan," Linda retorted. "You know you were."

Danny's eyes twinkled. "You know, Jim, I thought you were getting a lot of special attention when the doctor was there."

"Aw."

"Can't say that I blame you for liking her. I'd say she was cute."

"She isn't my girlfriend or anything like that," Jim protested lamely. "We–we're just friends."

"I know. I know. You don't have to explain."

Jim slumped in the seat. "You get a guy all mixed up."

"Wait a minute. I'm not the one who made you so crazy that you tried to climb a tree and look in an eagle's nest," Danny told him.

Jim half turned in the seat and began to look out the window.

After a time Linda spoke. "We did have to go up to that stupid old camp," she grumbled. "It was the worst summer I have ever had. "

Jim's eyes twinkled, yet were serious. "Parts of it were tough, I've got to admit, but I sure learned what it is that keeps a missionary on the field. I'd give anything to work with people like those who took us in!"

THE DANNY ORLIS SERIES

The Danny Orlis series, by Bernard Palmer, delivers a blend of adventure, mystery, and suspense through various settings—from the Canadian wilderness to Guatemalan jungles. Danny Orlis, an adept outdoorsman, skilled athlete, and committed Christian, employs his quick thinking, calm bravery, and biblical solutions to confront everyday problems and hair-raising dangers. Early stories focus on Danny navigating school life, sports, and outdoor challenges, while in later books, Danny and his wife Kay provide wisdom and guidance to youngsters facing lifelike situations and challenges. Having sold over two million copies, this series has made Palmer a renowned author in Christian youth literature. Palmer is also the author of the Felicia Cartright series and various other series for Christian youth.